Who says he has to be Mr. Right? What's wrong with Mr. Right Now?

The world had narrowed to three things: Jace's mouth, Noelle's fingers and the half a cookie clutched between them.

His breath mingled with hers. "Are you ready?"

In a heartbeat, the cookie vanished from her hand and her index finger was drawn into the warm, wet vortex of his mouth. He worked his way down to her pinkie, tormenting each finger in turn with his lips, teeth and tongue until they were sucked clean.

Oh. My. God.

"I'm still hungry."

She glanced at the tin in her lap. "There're more cookies."

"That's not what I'm hungry for."

Jace plucked the tin of cookies off her lap and set it down on the bench behind him.

"I think you know what I want..."

Dear Reader,

Finally! You met the baby of the Nelson family, ballerina Noelle, in *Triple Threat*. Now, three books later, she gets her own story in *Triple Score*.

Things aren't all rosy for poor Noelle. She's torn her ACL, a possible career-ending injury for a ballet dancer. So she's holed up at an exclusive rehab center focused on one thing and one thing only—following her treatment plan and getting back onstage ASAP.

Enter bad-boy baseball player Jace Monroe. He's ruptured the ligament in his elbow—again—and he needs to get better fast so he can rejoin his team, the Sacramento Storm, as shortstop. But unlike Noelle, Jace isn't a by-the-books kind of guy. He's willing to break the rules of rehab to get what he wants. And what he wants is to play baseball—and tear down the walls the elusive, alluring ballerina keeps putting up between them.

I've loved my time with the Nelson family, and I hope you have, too. Sadly, *Triple Score* is the last in The Art of Seduction series. But you'll get the chance to catch up with all of the Nelson siblings in the epilogue. And you might get to see at least one Nelson pairing in one of my upcoming books for Harlequin Blaze. Remember Malcolm and Marisa from *Triple Threat*? Well, it looks as if they'll be getting their own story, a Christmas book tentatively titled *Six Pack Santa*.

But first you'll get to see more of Jace's pals Cooper and Reid. So play ball!

Until next time,

Regina

Regina Kyle

Triple Score

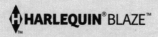

Recycling programs
for this product may
not exist in your area.

ISBN-13: 978-0-373-79910-7

Triple Score

Copyright © 2016 by Denise Smoker

Printed in U.S.A.

www.Harlequin.com

Regina Kyle was destined to be an author when she won a story contest at age eight with a touching tale about a squirrel and a nut pie. By day, she composes dry legal briefs. At night, she writes steamy romance with heart and humor. A lover of all things theatrical, Regina lives with her husband, teenage daughter and two melodramatic cats. When she's not writing, she's usually singing, reading, cooking or watching bad reality television.

Books by Regina Kyle

Harlequin Blaze

The Art of Seduction

Triple Threat
Triple Time
Triple Dare

To get the inside scoop on Harlequin Blaze and its talented writers, be sure to check out BlazeAuthors.com.

All backlist available in ebook format.

Visit the Author Profile page at Harlequin.com for more titles.

For Diane. My only sister, my first friend. I hope you read this under the covers with a flashlight and no one catches you and tells you to go to sleep. And that you like it as much as you did *Flat Stanley*. W2T, 143.

1

"THAT'S IT, JACE." A female voice, thick and smoky, drifted through the closed door. "Perfect."

A low, male moan followed. "Feels good."

"Not too hard. Just a little more."

"Oh, yeah."

Noelle Nelson froze, one hand on the grip of her crutch and the other inches from the door marked "Physical Therapy." The room was usually empty this time of night. But the couple in there clearly had a different kind of therapy session in mind.

Ewww.

She lowered her hand. Her nightly stretches would have to wait. She might not be able to do much with a torn knee ligament, but she'd be damned if she was going to let herself go. When her leg healed and she got the green light to dance again, she'd be ready. More than ready.

Noelle tightened her fists around the rubber crutch grips, fully intending to swing herself around and hobble back to her room. That was the right thing to do. Not lean in and press her ear to the door. But morbid curiosity wouldn't let her leave without at least trying to figure out who the heck was in there. Maybe she could pick up

a few pointers. It'd been a while since she'd gotten any action. Not that anyone at the rehab center had sparked her interest. No one had visions of mixing it up on the massage table dancing in her head.

"That's far enough." The woman's voice pitched higher.

"Come on," the man cajoled.

"Stop, Jace. I mean it."

"Just a little further. I promise."

"I said no."

WTF? Noelle pressed closer to the door, straining to hear better. No more protests. No sounds of a struggle. Just clanking metal, like someone was using the free weights.

What in God's green earth was going on in there?

She reached for the doorknob again. A little peek. That was all she needed to make sure the woman, whoever she was, was okay. Then she could walk—or limp—away with a clear conscience.

Noelle inched the knob to the right and pushed the door open a hair, then a bit more. Damn. Still not enough to see anything. She risked discovery and cracked the door open farther, leaning forward on her crutches to see far enough into the room to spot the mysterious Jace and his gal pal.

Finally, she caught a glimpse—two heads bent next to each other, one fair, one dark. She leaned in, holding her breath. One of her crutches wobbled. She grabbed at it, her pulse accelerating, but it slipped out from under her and clattered to the floor.

"Shit." Teetering, she reached for the closest thing to her—the door—to steady herself. Instead, it swung open and she tumbled through the opening. Trying to muster as much dancer's grace as she could, she threw

down her other crutch and thrust out her hands. They met the scratchy indoor-outdoor carpet of the physical therapy room with a jolt, blessedly taking the brunt of the impact. She collapsed in a heap, her injured leg, in a brace from mid-thigh to just below her knee, extended out behind her.

"Shit," she repeated, slowly raising her head and absorbing the scene in front of her. No strewn clothing. No naked bodies. No show of force. Nothing even remotely sexual or threatening. Just Sara, one of the therapists on staff, hovering over a man sitting on one of the exercise benches, all his energy focused on what looked to be a five-pound weight clutched in his fist.

And what a man.

Even with a brace from the middle of his upper arm to his wrist, Noelle could sense the power in his tattooed bicep. She'd spent her life being lifted and thrown by dancers toned and strong from intense, daily workouts. But they were more on the lean side. This guy was built like a linebacker, muscle on muscle on muscle. His tank top clung to his broad chest with well-defined pecs and his gym shorts hugged thighs he'd clearly spent hours bulking up with squats and lunges. Sweat beaded at the back of his bent head, dampening the thick, dark curls at the base of his neck, and he radiated a not-so-quiet determination.

"Ohmigod!" Sara's shout broke Noelle out of her lust-induced stupor. The therapist rushed over to her, moving immediately to kneel beside her. With practiced hands, she manipulated Noelle's injured leg, feeling up and down the brace. "Are you okay?"

"I think so." Noelle struggled to sit up. "Nothing hurt except my pride."

"Everything seems in place." Sara nodded reassuringly. "You're lucky."

Right. She'd just fallen flat on her face in front of the only guy to get her hormones to wake up and do the cha-cha since Yannick had dumped her in front of the entire company six months ago. Six lonely, sex-starved months. Real lucky.

"Don't move. Let me get an ice pack in case it starts to swell."

"I'm fine, really," Noelle insisted. "I don't want to interrupt your session."

"We're through here." Sara stood and shot Jace a warning look before crossing to the door. "Right?"

He shrugged and looked up, giving Noelle her first glimpse of eyes the color of fine, aged whiskey, tinged with what looked like concern. "If you say so."

"I do. I only agreed to stay late so you could get acclimated to the facilities here, not work yourself to death on your first day." Sara ducked into the hallway and Jace appeared in her place at Noelle's side, all six-foot-something of him occupying the air above her in a way the tiny therapist never could.

"Lose something?" He held Noelle's crutches out in front of him. Any concern she'd seen in those whiskey eyes had morphed into amusement.

"You could say that."

"I just did." He handed her crutches.

"Thanks." She grabbed them and tried—unsuccessfully—to get to her feet. Normally, she wouldn't disobey a direct order from her PT. And you didn't get more direct than, "Don't move." But she had to get out of there and away from Mr. Tall, Dark and Dangerous. Fast. Well, as fast as she could in her present condition.

"Hang on." The man in question reached down with

his good arm and took hold of her elbow. Arousal zinged down her forearm to her fingertips. "Here. Lean on me."

She shook him off, needing the tingles to stop. Six months celibate or not, she hadn't flown across the country for a casual hookup, no matter how hot she found the hook-ee. She was there for one reason and one reason only—to get back on stage as soon as humanly possible. "I'm perfectly capable of managing by myself."

"I'm sure you are." His fingers curled around her elbow again and damned if the tingles didn't start anew. "But why should you have to when you've got a strong, almost completely healthy male to help?"

Indeed.

"Fine." She swallowed, moistening lips suddenly drier than Arizona in August. "But watch out for the leg."

"Your wish is my command." He gave a mock bow, wrapped his good arm around her waist and lifted her gently, pulling her flush against all those warm, hard, beautiful muscles as she inched upward. He smelled like sweat and soap and strong, healthy male, and she fought the nervous shudder building up inside her.

This was a bad idea. No, not bad. Monumentally stupid. Like trapeze-without-a-net stupid.

"I've got it from here, thanks." She stuck a crutch under each arm and stood as tall as her injured leg would allow. "I'd shake your hand, but I'm not too steady on these things."

"You don't say." He crossed his arms in front of his chest and eyed her up and down, not bothering to hide the glint of raw appreciation in his gaze. "Explains why you fell through the door, landed on your ass and interrupted my workout."

More like on her face, but she wasn't about to correct him. Not when she was too busy trying to control her

cha-chaing hormones. "I didn't think anyone would be in here this late. I was planning on doing some stretches, but then I heard voices…"

"Eavesdropping?" A playful grin teased the corners of his lips. "Hear anything interesting?"

She pursed her lips. "If you must know, it sounded like you two were getting…intimate. And then Sara said stop, and you wouldn't, so I thought she might be…in trouble."

"In trouble?" A burst of laughter escaped him. "Get this straight, Duchess. I don't have to pressure women to be with me."

"I don't imagine you do," she muttered.

"So you opened the door for a little lookie-loo?" He waggled his brows. "I wouldn't have pegged you as a voyeur. Kinky. I like it."

"That's not how it was." She wobbled on her crutches, not sure whether to stay and continue what was turning into verbal foreplay or flee in search of Sara and the ice. Before she could make up her mind, he strode over to the weight rack, grabbed a ten pounder in each hand and began doing squats.

"Hey." She shuffled a couple of steps forward. "Sara said you were through for the night."

"She said we were through. And we are. I'm just doing a little leg work before bedtime. I don't care what those quacks in Sacramento think. I'm going to be back by the start of next season, better than ever."

"Next season?" She studied him. The shock of blue-black hair falling across his forehead. The full sleeves of tattoos, partially hidden by his brace. The logo of Thor brandishing a lightning bolt in one hand and a baseball bat in the other on his sweat-stained shirt. All of it clicked into place. "You're that baseball player. Jace Morgan. The one who hit for the cycle in last year's All-Star game."

Not that she had a clue what that meant. But the way her brother Gabe and his buddy Cade had gone on and on about it, it had to be pretty extraordinary.

"It's Monroe." He switched to lunges. "Want my autograph?"

"Dream on." What she wanted was him gone. She'd picked the Spaulding Center for Rehabilitation and Research because of its reputation for being discreet. With a star athlete like him there, the press was sure to come sniffing around. And just like that—poof—there went any shot she had of keeping her recovery on the downlow. The whole dance world would know where Noelle Nelson, prima ballerina of the New York City Ballet, had gone to mend her ruptured ACL. A dancer's worst nightmare.

She tightened her grip on her crutches and headed for the door.

"Leaving so soon?" Jace's tone was almost taunting.

Noelle clumped around to look at him. He was still lunging, his fine, firm ass squeezed tight, the muscles in his legs bunching and flexing with exertion. It was a second before she could remember what she was going to say. "Not every woman is susceptible to your charms."

Liar, liar, pointe shoes on fire.

He stopped lunging to smirk at her. "So you admit I have charms."

"I admit no such thing." She huffed a stray strand of long, blond hair off her face. The man was as annoying as he was attractive.

Jace shook his head and crossed to the weight rack, where he exchanged the two ten-pound dumbbells for one twenty pounder. "The lady doth protest too much, methinks."

"I do not—" She stopped midsentence, the irony of

her words not lost on her, and reached down to scratch an itch under her knee brace. "Shakespeare?"

"Not all jocks are dumb." He sat on the edge of the bench and started in on hammer curls with his good arm. So much for a little leg work. "There's more to me than meets the eye."

That was what she was afraid of.

"I think I could use that ice pack, after all. I'd better go see what's keeping Sara." She hobbled to the door.

"Hold up, Duchess." Jace set down the weight with a clank. "You know my name, but I don't know yours."

"Sucks for you," Noelle called over her shoulder without stopping her snail's-pace escape. He'd find out eventually. Bat his too-long eyelashes and worm it out of Sara or some unsuspecting nurse. Until then, he'd have to be satisfied with Duchess.

Because Noelle had a mission. And a plan. And neither one included a bad-boy ballplayer with a panty-melting smile and a working knowledge of the Bard.

Jace frowned and concentrated on the barbell in his hand, his reps picking up speed. He didn't want to think about Duchess What's-Her-Name and her ridiculous assumption that he was getting it on with his new PT. Or her legs that seemed to go on forever. Or the way her sweet little ass swayed when she hobbled out of the room. Who knew crutches could be sexy?

He had enough to worry about. He hadn't taken a three-and-a-half-hour flight—commercial, no less—to let himself be distracted by a pretty face and an even prettier body. He was going to be back in a Storm uniform by spring training, playing the best ball of his life.

He lowered the weight to the floor with a grimace and leaned forward, resting his forearms on his knees

and staring at his reflection in the mirror. The guy who looked back at him had never been afraid of a little hard work. Hell, it wasn't the first time he'd torn a ligament in his throwing arm. Been there, done that and he had come back in record time. But this time he'd needed surgery, and he'd be lying if he said the man in the mirror didn't look a little scared.

The pocket in his gym shorts buzzed and he pulled out his cell, glanced at the screen and swiped his finger across, grateful for the interruption. "Hey, dude. Tough loss."

On the other end of the line, Cooper Morgan, Sacramento Storm second baseman, swore. "Yeah. The close ones really suck. How's the rehab going?"

Slow. Painful. "Great. I'll be back at short before you know it."

"Not until next season." A note of caution crept into Cooper's voice. He and Jace were part of the trio the press dubbed "the most lethal double play combo in the major leagues," and he'd always been the level-headed one. "The good, the bad and the ugly," a reporter had called them. Cooper was the "good," Jace the "bad" and first baseman Reid Montgomery, with a jagged scar across one cheek that made him look a modern-day pirate, the "ugly."

"I know. I heard the damn doctors."

"I'm sure you heard them. But are you actually going to listen for a change?"

"Who appointed you my goddamn keeper?"

"It was either me or Reid." Jace could hear the smile in his friend's voice. "And he's got some new chick he's into, so…"

Jace chuckled and reached down to grab the water bottle he'd stashed under the bench. "Say no more. Let

me guess. Tall, blond and drop dead gorgeous, with an IQ only slightly higher than her waist measurement."

Cooper's answering chuckle echoed over the phone. "Bingo."

Like the Duchess. Except for the IQ thing. Jace could tell from her quick barbs she had more going on upstairs than Reid's usual companions.

Beauty and brains. A dangerous combination.

Jace took a gulp of water and swirled it around in his mouth before letting it trickle down his throat. "So what's the deal? You still coming out here for the All Star break?"

"Wouldn't miss it for the world. Think they'll let you out for a day or two?"

"I don't see why not." Jace sipped the water again and closed his eyes, letting his head fall back. "As long as I'm a good boy."

"You?" Cooper scoffed. "Not likely."

"I can be good," Jace insisted. "When I want to be."

"Which, unfortunately, isn't often."

"Did you call to harass me or was there something you wanted?" Jace chugged the last of his water and wiped his mouth on his good arm.

"To harass you."

"Mission accomplished." Jace stood and stretched. "I better go. Rumor has it they get pissed around here if you're not in bed by ten."

"Are you at rehab or summer camp?"

"Both." Jace bent to pick up the weight. "I'll call you in a few days. Kick some ass for me in St. Louis."

"You bet."

Jace ended the call, returned the weight to its place on the rack and headed back to his room. Once inside, he flipped on the light switch and stared, open-mouthed.

"What the hell?"

The bed had been empty when he left to meet Sara. Now one of those inflatable love dolls lay sprawled on top, her cherry-tipped breasts pointed straight up at the ceiling and her ruby red mouth in a permanent O. A cardboard box sat between her open legs. On one side, the words For Your Enjoyment: Handle With Care were printed in bold, bright blue marker. No return address, but the postmark was from Chicago, where the Storm had finished up a recent road trip.

Jace flicked open the utility knife on his key chain, sliced through the packing tape and began pulling out items one by one. A box of condoms. A tube of Astroglide. He kept digging. The damn thing was packed with enough sex toys to keep a rowdy bachelorette party whooping it up for hours.

Cooper and Reid's warped idea of a care package. They'd probably paid some gullible orderly a fortune to do their dirty work. Or maybe offered him box seats the next time the Storm were in Phoenix.

"Very funny, assholes."

The corners of Jace's lips curled into a smile in spite of himself. It *was* funny. Though God only knew what the staff would think when they came to clean in the morning.

He started chucking stuff back in the box until all that was left was the doll. No way was she going to fit, not in her present state. And he sure as hell wasn't leaving her like that. With a sigh, Jace opened the valve.

Nothing.

He picked up the doll and squeezed it. A long, slow whoosh of air escaped from the valve. He squeezed again. "Come on, baby. Give it to me."

A shrill, female squeak from behind him made Jace turn toward the door, the doll still in his arms.

"Sorry." Noelle leaned against the door jamb, almost as if her crutches weren't enough to keep her vertical. Her porcelain cheeks tinted red. "Again."

"Back for some more covert operations?" Jace loosened his hold on the doll. "Has anyone ever told you your timing sucks?"

"Maybe it's not my timing." Her eyes traveled from him to the doll and back again. "Maybe it's your…libido."

"Very funny." He smiled in spite of himself. She was smart, sassy and not in the least bit intimidated by his tattoos or his attitude or his fame, like so many women. "You know there was nothing going on between me and Sara."

"That doesn't explain you and…" she wagged a finger at the doll "…her."

"A practical joke from a couple of friends."

"Some friends."

He threw the doll onto the floor and stepped on it, squashing one plastic boob. The air came out in a hiss, and he continued to flatten the doll with his feet.

"You're going to pop it."

He raised an eyebrow. "Do I look like I care?"

"You never know. You might need her for…something."

"Like I said, I've never been that hard up for female companionship. And I don't plan to start now."

"From the way things looked a minute ago, you could have fooled me."

He stopped his rhythmic stomping to stare at her. "Was there a reason for this late-night visit? Couldn't sleep? Lonely? Miss me, maybe?"

Her face flushed an ever deeper scarlet. "Sara said I should apologize for spying on you guys."

He rolled his eyes. "Not much of an apology if she's making you do it."

"I'm here, aren't I?" she huffed. "And no one's holding a gun to my back."

"Well?" He folded his arms across his chest.

"Well, what?"

"I'm waiting." She narrowed her eyes at him, and he tilted his head. "For your apology."

"You really are the most infuriating man." Her lower lip jutted out into a pout that he shouldn't have found so sexy.

"I've heard." He shrugged. "Many times. But I'm not the one who has something to apologize for."

"All right, I'm sorry. I shouldn't have listened in. And I shouldn't have jumped to conclusions." Her aqua eyes flashed with righteous indignation. "Are you satisfied?"

"Hardly." He picked up the deflated doll, stuffed it into the box and closed the lid before she could get a glimpse of any of the other goodies inside. "But it'll do. For now."

"Forever," she countered as she turned to leave. "I'm here to get back on my feet, not make friends."

"We'll see about that, Duchess." He frowned, realizing he still didn't know her damn name, and watched, transfixed by the swaying of her perfect ass as she disappeared out the door. The squeak of her crutches on the linoleum of the hallway echoed in her wake. "We'll see."

He tossed the box onto the floor and stretched out on his bed, the room strangely empty without her larger-than-life presence. He liked sparring with her. She was a worthy opponent and a certified babe to boot, with eyes a guy could get lost in, hair that begged to be mussed and a body built for sin. And she'd made him forget for

a moment, had briefly lifted the tension that had gripped his chest since he went down on the field.

He smiled and reached for the TV remote. Maybe rehab didn't have to be a total drag. All work and no play made Jace a dull boy.

And if there was one thing he wasn't, it was dull.

2

THE CLOCK ON the wall read 11:15 when Jace sauntered into the PT room the next morning. A full 45 minutes before his session was scheduled. No one would mind if he did a little cardio first, right?

Wrong.

"What are you doing here?" Sara rushed over to him before he could even put down his water bottle. "Your appointment's not until noon."

"I wanted to get some time in on the treadmill."

"No way." Sara shook her head. "I don't want you jarring that elbow until it's more stable."

"It's in a brace, for Christ's sake." Jace looked at his arm, the joint in question almost immobile thanks to the range-of-motion splint, and scowled. "How much more stable can it get?"

"You just got here yesterday." She pursed her lips. "I haven't had a chance to fully assess it yet."

He held up his arm. "Assess away."

"I have other patients to deal with right now." She waved a hand around the room. A handful of other residents were using the equipment. One in particular caught

his attention—a very familiar one on a stationary bike in the far corner, her ponytail swinging as she pedaled.

He registered the empty treadmill beside her and grinned. Like Hannibal Smith, leader of the A-team, he loved it when a plan came together. "How come she gets to work out?"

"Because she's been here for a few weeks already. Today's her first day off crutches." Sara looked from Jace to the blonde, then back again. "And she's taking it easy. She follows instructions. Unlike some people."

"Hey, I can follow instructions." Never mind that he'd completely ignored them last night. "When I have to."

She smirked. "You forget I have your records from the hospital in California."

Yeah. He hadn't exactly been a hit with the staff there. Noncompliant, they'd labeled him. Uncooperative. He preferred to think of himself as focused. Goal oriented. "What if I promise to go slow, like the Duchess?"

"The Duchess?" Sara's brows knotted together.

Damn. He hadn't meant to let that slip.

"Yeah. She seems kind of…prissy. What's she in for? Fall off her high heels? Get trampled by crazed shoppers at the Macy's one-day sale?"

"You don't have any idea who she is, do you?" Sara jabbed a finger at his chest. "That's Noelle Nelson."

Finally. The Duchess had a name. "Is that supposed to mean something to me?"

"She's only like the most famous ballerina in the country. Maybe even the world. Principal dancer with the New York City Ballet."

Ballet? Jace knew as much about ballet as he did about nuclear physics. But he knew you needed two fully functioning knees. And from the look of the contraption on

Noelle's leg, she was in the same boat as him where her career was concerned. Without a paddle.

He watched her as she pedaled, her mouth set in a harsh line, a bead of sweat forming on her temple, her knuckles white on the handlebars. As slow as she was going, it still took an emotional toll. "Shit."

"Yeah, shit." Sara gave him a not-so-gentle shove toward the treadmill. "Go. Walk. But if I see you doing anything more than that, I'm hitting the emergency stop button."

"Deal." Jace started to offer his hand to her but pulled it back. "I'd shake on it, but I wouldn't want to jar anything."

"Ha-ha." Sara picked up a physioball and headed across the room, where an older man with one ankle wrapped was sitting on a mat next to a set of low parallel bars. "I'll come get you when it's time for your session."

Jace set off in the opposite direction.

"Morning, Duchess." He plunked his water bottle into the holder on the treadmill console. "Fancy meeting you here."

She stared out the window, not so much as glancing at him. "I thought we agreed to steer clear of each other."

"You agreed. I just smiled." He flashed her another of his never-fail-to-charm grins and hit the start button on the treadmill, setting the speed as high as he could without incurring the wrath of Sara.

"If you have to work out next to me, could you at least keep your mouth shut?"

"I thought we'd chit-chat. Get to know each other. Pass the time. Hell, at this speed, I could recite the Gettysburg Address." He peeked over his shoulder for Sara. Her back to him, she was totally occupied with the guy

in the ankle wrap. He edged the rate of the treadmill up a notch. "If I remembered it."

Noelle swiveled her head to look at him. Finally. Too bad her baby blues flashed with annoyance and not a more...pleasurable emotion. Like desire. "What part of 'I'm not here to make friends' did you not get?"

"You can't have too many friends. And you know what they say about all work and no play."

"Well, I don't want to play." Her head snapped forward, her attention back on the window, or whatever lay outside it. "You're not the only one with a job on the line and people counting on you."

"Sara says you're some big-time ballerina."

"Sara's new. She talks too much."

"What'd you do?" He gestured toward her leg. "Torn ACL?"

"How did you guess?"

"I've seen a few in my time. Not on a dancer, though."

"Dancers are just as much athletes as baseball players." From the way the last two words dripped off her tongue, it was clear she considered his profession on par with used car salesmen and politicians. "More so, if you asked me. You don't see us sitting on the bench, spitting tobacco. And the guys I work with throw around hundred-pound ballerinas, not a five ounce sphere."

"Easy, Duchess." He held up a palm. "I wasn't trying to insult you."

"You don't have to try." She tossed her ponytail. "You just do."

"Like Yoda?"

"Minus the green skin and the pointy ears, obviously."

"So you think dancers are better athletes than ball-players?"

"Not better." Wrinkles creased her forehead like she

was deep in thought, searching for the right word to bridge the gap between her occupation and his. "Different. But we earn our living with our bodies, just like you do."

"Finally." He flashed another mega-watt smile, with as little effect as the last one. Damn. He hadn't struck out this many times in a row since he'd faced Johan Santana at Shea his rookie season. "Something we have in common."

"I seriously doubt there's anything else."

"Do you?" He raised an eyebrow.

"Let's just say I'm not interested in finding out." She slowed, then stopped pedaling.

"That's disappointing."

"I guess you'll have to learn to live with disappointment."

She eased herself off the bike and made her way over to the free weights. He shrugged off her pissy attitude, knowing from personal experience she was covering for something. Like the fear of losing a lifetime of hard work.

Besides, it was just as well. If their conversation had gone on any longer, he might have let slip just how well acquainted he was with disappointment.

"What the hell?"

He stumbled as the treadmill came to a stop. Sara stood next to the machine, her finger still on the e-stop button. "I warned you."

"I was barely moving."

"You were practically running." She handed him a towel. "It's time for your session. Wipe off your machine and let's get going. You're in my army now, hotshot."

Great. Not even noon and he'd already managed to

piss off two women. With a groan, he balled up the towel, tossed it into a nearby hamper and followed Sara.

It was gonna be a fan-freaking-tabulous day.

WHAT WAS IT about Jace Monroe that brought out her inner diva?

Noelle flopped onto her bed, if you could call gingerly lowering herself so as to avoid jolting her bum-knee flopping. She really should take a shower, but she didn't have the energy after her workout. Half an hour on a stupid stationary bike, and she felt as spent as if she'd danced Aurora in *Sleeping Beauty*. Plus, she was supposed to Skype with Holly in—she glanced at the digital clock on her nightstand—ten minutes.

Fuming, she ran a brush through her hair in a futile attempt to look presentable and pulled her laptop out from under the bed. Why did she let him get to her? She'd dealt with plenty of macho morons who saw ballet as some sort of sissy thing. One fairly innocuous comment from Jace, and she'd flown off the handle.

The guy must think she was a lunatic. Not that she cared what he thought. Not one bit.

Now she just had to convince her brain, which seemed to be fixated on him. And her heart, which beat a little faster every time he looked at her with that maddeningly sexy, Patrick-Swayze-in-*Dirty-Dancing* smile.

She shrugged it off and booted up the computer. Nothing like a little time with her sister and niece to get her mind off bedroom eyes, sun-kissed skin and sculpted muscles, three things she didn't need occupying valuable brain space. No, what she needed now was to be totally focused on her rehabilitation. Without that, her chances of dancing professionally again were next to nil.

She'd just logged onto Skype when an alert flashed

showing an incoming call. She clicked on "answer with video," and a live feed of Holly popped up, a squirming, curly-haired toddler in her arms.

"Hey, Hols." Noelle settled in on the bed, adjusting the laptop across her knees so her own face showed in a box on the corner of the screen. "How's my baby girl?"

"Fast." Holly untangled a chubby fist from her hair and handed her daughter a ring of plastic keys, which she immediately began chewing on. "And sneaky. I'm exhausted. It's like she started walking and hasn't stopped. Yesterday, I turned my back for a second and she figured out how to open the sliding glass door. She was halfway to the lake before I caught her."

Noelle's gaze drifted to her brace then back to the computer. "Maybe she can give me a few pointers."

"Rehab not going well?" Holly asked, bouncing the toddler on her own perfectly healthy knee.

"Rehab's rehab. Two hours a day of torture to move an inch forward." Noelle ran a hand through her still sweat-dampened hair. "I just want to be back on stage, as soon as possible."

"Have the doctors given you any idea when that might be?"

"No." What she didn't want to admit—to Holly or herself—was that the question wasn't so much when as it was if. "They're telling me to take it one day at a time. Easy for them to say. It's not their life on hold."

"You're more than your career, Noe."

"I know." And she did. Really. For her, ballet wasn't about the bright lights, the elaborate costumes or the thundering applause. It was about the dancing, pure and simple. Something she'd done each day, every day since she was just a few years older than her niece. And if she didn't have that...

She pasted on a smile. Things were treading dangerously close to *The Turning Point* territory. Accentuate the positive, her mother always said. "I'm off the crutches."

"That's a good sign, right?"

"So they say. I'm putting weight on it. Even rode the stationary bike today." She conveniently left out the fact that she'd practically passed out afterward.

"If anyone can come back from this, you can," Holly insisted. "I've never known anyone as fearless as you, especially when it comes to your dancing. Remember how you convinced Mom and Dad to let you take the subway into New York for lessons? Alone? At thirteen?"

"It helped that I was the baby. By the time I was a teenager, you, Gabe and Ivy had already broken them down."

"Down." A tiny toddler voice echoed through the computer's tinny speakers. "Down."

"Nick," Holly called, struggling to hold on to her fidgety daughter. "Can you come and take Joy?"

A second later the handsome face of Holly's moviestar husband appeared over her shoulder. "Hey, Noelle. Fighting the good fight?"

Noelle nodded. "Always."

"Here." Holly placed Joy into Nick's waiting arms, her nose wrinkling. "I think she needs a fresh diaper."

"I got this." He hoisted Joy into the crook of one arm and looked straight into the camera. "Hang tough, sis. We're all rooting for you."

"Thanks, bro. See you at Thanksgiving?"

"If not before. Enjoy your girl chat."

He bent to place a quick, tender kiss on Holly's forehead, and not for the first time Noelle felt a pang of longing for all she'd sacrificed at the altar of ballet. Home. Husband. Kids. She couldn't even have a pet, for Christopher's sake. She'd tried once—a Yorkie she named Sous-

Sus—and it had been a total disaster. Traveling with a dog, even a small one, had turned out to be a logistical nightmare. How Kelly Clarkson and Taylor Swift managed it was beyond her. She'd wound up giving Sous-Sus to her hairstylist, who was lucky enough to have a rent-controlled apartment within spitting distance of Central Park.

"Come on, pumpkin." Nick's voice brought her back to the present and the computer screen. He had shifted his attention to his daughter, tweaking her button nose. "We've got a diaper to change."

They disappeared from view, leaving Holly alone on the screen. "Now that it's just us gals over legal age, how about we talk about something more fun. Like boys."

"You're trying to take my mind off the fact that I'm basically an unemployed invalid for the next who-knows-how-many months."

"Is it working?"

"Not really." Noelle flexed her feet and grimaced, even that tiny motion straining her overtired knee. "Besides, there's not much in the way of prime man meat around this place."

"Liar."

"I am not lying."

"Are, too." Holly crossed her arms in front of her chest. "You've got a tell."

"What do you mean?"

"Every time you lie, you tilt your head to one side. Usually the right. How do you think Mom knew you were the one who borrowed—" she put the word in air quotes "—her cashmere sweater and put it back with a huge stain on the sleeve?"

"I figured you told her."

"So who is he?" Holly asked, refusing to be diverted. "Is he hot? I need the dirty deets."

"You're married to *People*'s Sexiest Man Alive."

"And we have a toddler who doesn't like to sleep in her own bed. I have to live vicariously through you, at least until we get through the terrible twos."

Noelle snickered. "Well, I hate to disappoint you, but he's definitely not into me."

Not after she'd humiliated herself not once but twice by bursting in on him. And then been a total biatch to him on the bike.

"Ah ha!" Holly snapped her fingers. "So there is a he."

Oops. And people thought Gabe was the master of cross-examination. Poor Joy didn't stand a chance of getting away with anything as a teenager.

"Don't get excited. We're more like squabbling siblings than star-crossed lovers."

"Who is he?"

"Some hotshot baseball player. Jace something-or-another."

"Jace Monroe?" Holly squealed. "Oh my God, he's totally gorgeous, if you go for the whole tatted-up, boy-from-the-wrong-side-of-the-tracks thing. Which you do."

"How do you even know who he is?" Noelle rolled her eyes. "You hate baseball."

"Nick's a huge Storm fan from his time in California. He watches all their games on the MLB network." Holly reached out of the frame to grab a Diet Coke. "But this conversation isn't about me and Nick. It's about you and Jace. What makes you think he's not into you?"

Noelle propped up the pillow behind her and leaned back against the headboard, juggling the computer on her lap so she stayed on camera. "You wouldn't believe it."

"Try me."

While Holly sipped her soda, Noelle spilled the whole, sordid story, from interrupting what she thought was a sexual encounter to the love doll incident, ending with how she'd given him the cold shoulder in the gym that morning. When she finished, Holly clucked her tongue.

"You need a do-over. Apologize to him again. And get it right this time."

"I had a feeling you'd say that."

"So what are you waiting for? Hang up and say you're sorry to that beautiful hunk of man."

"I'm afraid of what I might walk in on." Noelle laughed a little too loud, trying to hide the fact that her words had conjured images of Jace in all kinds of compromising—and mostly naked—positions. "I don't exactly have the best track record where he's concerned."

"Aha," Holly nodded and her lips curved knowingly. "Now I understand."

"Understand what?"

"You'll find out soon enough."

"No, I won't." Noelle smacked a palm down on the bedside table. "I can't afford to get sidetracked by some charmer in a muscle tee and athletic shorts. I'm fighting for my career here, Hols."

"What good's a career without someone to come home to?"

"I'm not looking for a life partner. I've got all I can handle right now."

"Okay, then. Who says he has to be Mr. Right? What's wrong with Mr. Right Now? You're young. Let loose. Live a little." A baby's cry made Holly startle, and she sighed. "I've gotta go. Nick's a magician with his hands, but give him a diaper and he falls apart."

"TMI, big sis. TMI."

Holly chuckled. "Think about what I said. And call me when you and Mr. MVP kiss and make up."

"We're not going to…"

But Holly's smiling face had already disappeared from the computer screen. And Noelle wasn't any closer to figuring out how she was going to coexist for the next few weeks with the sexiest shortstop in the southwest without making a total fool out of herself again.

Or jumping his oh-so-fine bones.

3

"In baseball, the Storm trounced St. Louis 11–3 behind the red-hot bat of rookie phenom Dean Hafler. Hafler's been on fire since taking over for injured starting short-stop Jace Monroe, hitting .327 with runners in scoring position. He's settled down in the field, too, playing error-free defense in his last six games."

"Effing Sportscenter." Jace jabbed a finger at the power button on the remote, but the commentator droned on.

"Monroe reinjured his UCL in last month's series against Philadelphia, and it's uncertain when—or if—he'll return. Sources close to the team say even with Monroe healthy, Hafler's stats may put him in the running for the starting job next season."

"Sources, my ass." No doubt Hafler's barracuda of an agent had floated that rumor, trying to up his client's ante in the free-agent market in the off season. Jace threw the remote down, stalked over to the television and turned it off. "The only way that little pissant's gonna steal my job is over my dead body."

Jace snatched his cell off the nightstand. He needed some air and to have a good, long talk with his own

worthless agent. He had a few questions that needed answering—like why the hell was he hearing this shit on ESPN and not from the guy he paid to protect his career.

He pulled open the door, already hitting his agent's speed dial, and almost plowed into Noelle.

"Bad time?" She stood with her fist raised to knock on the door he'd flung open. He found himself hoping she'd drop her palm on his chest, let its heat scorch through the well-worn cotton of his favorite T-shirt, right over the word *guy* in I'm the Guy Your Mother Warned You About. Instead, it fell to her side, a smile playing around the corners of her mouth. "Again? I thought the third time was supposed to be the charm."

He pressed the end-call button, stuck the phone in his back pocket and leaned against the door frame. "No PT. No sex toys. Just me, about to go for a walk."

"Can I join you?" The way she moistened her lips told him she was nervous, although it didn't shed any light on why. But that didn't stop his dick from twitching as her tongue darted out again. "I'm not exactly up to warp speed, but the doctors say I need to start moving around more now that I've lost the crutches."

He stuffed a hand in the pocket of his jeans, hoping to hide what was sure to be a monster erection if he didn't get the damn thing under control, and fast. "I can't guarantee I'll be good company."

"Bad company's better than no company. And everybody else in this place is either still going through puberty or over sixty."

"Meaning?" His eyes narrowed.

"Meaning I'm going stir-crazy, and I need someone to share these with." She produced a tin from behind her back.

"What's in there?"

She jiggled the tin and the contents rattled. "Contraband."

He crossed his arms in front of his chest. "Drugs? Laundered money? An AK-47?"

"Better." She cracked the lid and held the tin under his nose. He smelled almonds and something he thought was coconut. "My mom's homemade macaroons. Strictly off-limits under the rehab diet. I was hoping they'd convince you to give me another shot at apologizing."

"Apology accepted." He pushed off the door frame, closing the door behind him. His agent could wait. He wasn't about to turn down a beautiful blonde, especially one bearing baked goods. "Come on. I know the perfect spot to enjoy them undetected."

She snapped the lid of the tin shut and followed him down the hall toward the reception area. He slowed, shortening his steps so she could keep up with him.

"Hold it right there." The nurse manning the main desk abandoned her post and jumped in front of them, one hand outstretched like a traffic cop or a member of the Supremes. "Where do you two think you're going?"

"Easy, Nurse Ratched." Jace softened the jab with his never-fail-to-charm-their-pants-off smile—if you didn't count Noelle—and snaked an arm around the ballerina's waist. "We're only going for a walk."

Noelle not-so-subtly elbowed him in the ribs.

"It's okay, Connie. Now that I'm off crutches, the doctors want me to work the kinks out of this thing." She tapped the brace covering her knee. "I promise we won't go far."

"Stay on the grounds." Connie let them pass.

"Thanks, doll," Jace called over his shoulder as he steered Noelle to the exit. "Don't wait up."

"Nice try," Connie hollered back. "But if you're not back by curfew, I'm calling in the search dogs."

"Great. I love dogs." The automatic doors slid open, blasting Jace with a burst of Arizona air, still hot even with the sun low on the horizon.

"Where's this so-called perfect spot?" Noelle asked after they'd walked a few feet.

"Don't knock it until you see it." He guided her onto a concrete path that ran alongside a man-made pond before disappearing down a hill into a strand of acacia. "And it's just past those trees."

At least it was two years ago.

"You weren't very nice to Connie," Noelle scolded.

"Connie's okay." His voice cracked on the last syllable. Damned if Noelle's schoolmarm tone didn't get him hotter than center field at Wrigley in July. He cleared his throat and started again. "We go way back. She'd be disappointed if I didn't mess with her."

"Old flame?" Noelle eyed him suspiciously.

"Not even close." They rounded a corner at the bottom of the hill and he led her to a wooden bench on the other side of the trees. Just as he'd remembered it, down to the sun-faded, weather-worn slats still needing a fresh coat of paint. "She was here the last time I was in."

He sat, patting the spot next to him. She followed suit, stretching her bad leg out in front of her. "The last time?"

He nodded, lifted his elbow, then let it fall. "This is my second stint with this thing. Tore it two years ago and got away without going under the knife. Not so lucky this time."

Her eyes filled with a pity he didn't deserve and sure as hell didn't want, especially from her. "I'm sorry."

"Don't be." He scuffed the ground in front of him with the toe of his Vans. "Odds are it'll be stronger than ever."

"Good."

He liked that she didn't ask questions or spout any of the bullshit he'd heard every day since his injury: "It could be worse," or "You'll be back out there sooner than you know it." And his favorite, "A million guys would kill to have the career you've had."

Assholes. Like he didn't know how lucky he'd been. Like he was a greedy bastard for wanting more.

"So how about those cookies?" He gestured toward the tin. She popped the lid and they each took a macaroon. He bit through the crisp shell and was instantly rewarded with a burst of moist, coconutty goodness.

"Damn, your mom can bake," he mumbled through a mouthful of cookie.

"She's Italian," Noelle said, as if that explained everything. And, in a way, it did. His mom's idea of preparing a meal had involved a takeout menu and a cell phone. At least he hadn't missed her cooking when she'd ditched him and his dad for greener pastures.

He reached for another and they ate in silence for a few minutes, the only sound their chewing, interrupted periodically by his moans of pleasure.

"Ballet did this, huh?" He nodded at her knee, extended in front of her.

She put the tin down on the bench between them. "We're not going there again, are we?"

"I never went there in the first place." He grabbed another cookie and stuffed it into his mouth. "I'm an athlete. But you—I watched you. You're an athlete and an artist."

"You...watched me?"

"You can find just about anything on YouTube these days."

She winced. "Then I suppose you saw the video of my accident. It's got over a million hits. Seems people enjoy

watching the suffering of others. The Germans even have a word for it. Schadenfreude."

"I don't know about the Germans, but I don't get my jollies by seeing folks in pain." He tapped his brace. "I tore this in front of 40,000 people at Citizens Bank Park. Had to be escorted off the field."

"Ouch."

"You said it."

"And I thought twenty-five hundred witnesses at Lincoln Center was bad. That calls for another cookie."

She held up a macaroon, but instead of taking it from her he leaned forward and bit into it, his lips brushing her fingertips. The contact sent a buzz of lust through him, and he jerked back.

"No good?" she asked, her voice husky. Her tongue darted out to moisten her lips and his cock swelled.

"To the contrary." His voice matched hers. "A little too good."

"The cookie? Or...?" Her hand still hung midair, clutching the remains of the macaroon.

"Or." He took hold of her wrist and brought her hand to his mouth. "If you don't want me to eat that damn cookie right out of your pretty little fingers then suck them into my mouth one by one, licking off every last crumb, stop me now."

Her eyes darkened to the navy blue of the Yankees logo. "And if I do?"

He nipped her fingertips. "Then sit back, relax and enjoy the ride."

RELAX? HE WANTED her to relax? Who was he kidding?

If pressing against him as he'd helped her up in the gym had been trapeze-without-a-net stupid, then this

was Russian-roulette reckless. But Holly's words echoed in her head.

Let loose. Live a little. Who says he has to be Mr. Right? What's wrong with Mr. Right Now?

Her lips parted and she had trouble focusing her gaze. Her palms itched with the need to grab his asinine I'm the Guy Your Mother Warned You About T-shirt and pull him to her, forcing his actions to speak louder than his deliciously dirty words. The world had narrowed to three things: his mouth, her fingers and the half a cookie between them.

"I'm going to count to three." His breath mingled with hers. "Are you ready?"

She nodded.

"One."

She swallowed hard.

"Two."

She closed her eyes.

"Three."

In a heartbeat, the cookie vanished from her hand and her index finger was drawn into the warm, wet vortex of his mouth. He worked his way down to her pinkie, tormenting each finger in turn with his lips, teeth and tongue until they were sucked clean.

"There." With one last lick, Jace released her hand, and it flopped into her lap like a newborn kitten. "All gone."

Zip-a-dee-doo-dah.

Noelle wasn't promiscuous, but she wasn't a sexual novice, either. How had she gone so long without experiencing…that? She shivered, picked up the tin of cookies and snapped the lid back on.

"Wait. You've got a few crumbs. Right—" he pointed to the corner of her mouth "—there."

She lifted her hand to her lips, but he caught it, stopping her.

"What are you doing?" Every last one of her nerve endings hummed with anticipation.

"I'm still hungry." He brought her hand down but didn't relinquish it, instead stroking slow circles on the inside of her wrist with his thumb.

She glanced at the tin in her lap. "There are more cookies."

"That's not what I'm hungry for." He plucked the tin off her lap and set it down on the bench behind him. "I think you know what I want."

Yeah, she did. And she wanted it, too. Trouble was she knew exactly what path it was going to lead her down— and what would be waiting for her at the end.

Heartache.

Loneliness.

And, if she was really lucky, a big, steaming serving of humiliation.

Exactly what she'd been left with when Yannick called it quits. Unless she could somehow manage to engage her body without engaging her heart, something other women seemed to have mastered but she could never figure out how to accomplish.

Live a little, Holly's voice echoed again. *What's wrong with Mr. Right Now?*

"I repeat." He raised his good hand and tangled his fingers in her hair. "If you don't want this, stop me now."

She couldn't if she tried.

So she didn't.

He pulled her in and he crushed his lips against hers. Not shy or tentative, this kiss was like the man himself— hot and hard, forcing the air from her lungs. It demanded

a response that she gave willingly, opening her mouth so he could slide his tongue inside.

He tasted good. Like coconut and almond from the macaroons but somehow better, as if their sweetness was mixed with the spice of wild, hungry sex. Sex the likes of which she'd never experienced, that would leave her breathless and panting and begging for more.

Her tongue met his and she melted into him, wanting—needing—more. Her fingers clutched at the soft cotton of his shirt and she moaned into his mouth. She couldn't recall ever feeling so wanton, so desperate. Whether it was due to the man or her six months of celibacy, she didn't know.

Beneath her hand, the muscles of his chest tightened, making her breath hitch. Who was she kidding? She knew damn well. It was the man.

He broke off the kiss, leaving her momentarily bereft until he worked his lips over her chin, down her neck, to the hollow of her throat, leaving a warm, wet trail in his wake. She tilted her head, encouraging him to explore further, just in time to catch of glimpse of something moving in the trees past his shoulder.

"Wait." She stiffened, listening, her eyes straining to see in the fading sunlight.

"Don't tell me you're having second thoughts now," he groaned against her skin, his mouth pushing past the neckline of her peasant blouse to skim the top of her breast. "Just when it was getting good."

She thought it was already pretty damn good, but there wasn't time to argue. "There's something—or someone—out there."

"Probably an animal." He moved to the other breast without missing a beat.

"You don't understand." The flutters in her stomach

traveled lower even as she pushed him away. "What if it's one of the nurses? Or another patient?"

He raised his head to pin her with a heavy-lidded stare. "Embarrassed to be seen with me, Duchess?"

"Ohmigod, what if it's the paparazzi?" she asked in a whisper, ignoring his question. They'd had a field day with her and Yannick's messy split, half of them painting her as a naive girl caught under the spell of her older, more experienced choreographer and the other half making it look like she was an opportunistic fame-seeker willing to screw anyone who could help her on her way up the ballet pyramid. And Yannick was a D-lister compared to Jace. If the press got wind of this…

A squirrel darted out from the trees, cocked its fuzzy little head at them and scampered off in the opposite direction from where Jace and Noelle had come.

"There's your paparazzi." Jace smirked. "Looks like your reputation is safe."

"For now. That was too close for comfort." She rose unsteadily and adjusted her blouse, struggling to tamp down the desire still thrumming through her veins. "We have to get out of here."

"What's the matter?" He joined her standing. "Never made out *al fresco* before?"

"Not usually, no."

He made a show of bowing to her, bending low with a flourish of his good wrist. "Then I'm flattered to be the man who persuaded you to change that."

"One kiss does not a habit break." She pulled a hair tie out of the pocket of her jean shorts and tamed her lust-mussed locks into a ponytail. "It was a…"

"Don't you dare say 'mistake.'" His gaze slipped down to the obvious bulge under the zipper of his Lucky's.

"Whatever the hell that was, it was definitely not a mistake."

"Fine." She looked away from his erection, heat creeping up her cheeks, and ambled as fast as her bad leg would take her up the path to the relative safety and privacy of her room. Jace caught up to her after a few steps. "I won't say it."

But that didn't mean it wasn't true. The man was like her own personal Kryptonite. Powerful, dangerous, hypnotic. She'd have to try all the harder to stay away from him or be rendered completely and utterly helpless to resist his hard-bodied, tatted-up, bad-boy spell.

4

"GREAT JOB TODAY." Sara took the barbell from Jace's hand and replaced it with a towel. "I'll see you tomorrow. Same bat time, same bat channel."

He wiped his forehead and slung the towel around his neck. "What the hell. It's not like I've got anything better to do."

Wasn't that the truth. He'd thought things were looking up after his cookie swap with Noelle. Sure, the lady protested. But her body hadn't thought their kiss was a mistake.

Instead, he'd barely seen Noelle since the infamous macaroon incident. No pouty lips. No perky breasts. No...

"Earth to Jace." Sara snapped her fingers in front of his face. "Scram. My next appointment's due any minute. You can do a half hour of cardio on the treadmill or the elliptical if you want, but no more than that and not too fast. The idea's to get your heart rate into the target zone, not keep going until you drop."

"Yes, ma'am." He stood and wiped down the utility bench he'd been using with the clean end of his towel. "Who's up next?"

If the week's pattern held, it wouldn't be Noelle. He didn't have any proof, but he had a strong suspicion she'd been scheduling her training sessions to avoid running into him.

"New kid. High school pitching sensation. Lost his arm to a downed power line."

"That sucks." Inadequate, Jace knew, but accurate.

Sara eyed him. "On second thought, maybe you should stick around. He could use a little cheering up. A bona fide sports hero might be just the thing."

Jace scrunched the towel up in his hand. He'd never been comfortable with the whole hero-worship-role-model thing. Who the hell would want to emulate him? He wasn't fit to be anyone's hero. He drank too much, partied too hard. He was just a kid from a broken home on the wrong side of the tracks who'd been lucky enough to make it in the majors. End of story. "Some other time. I've got to hit the shower and make some phone calls."

"I'm holding you to that," Sara called after his retreating back.

"You do that." With a wave of his good arm, he pushed through the door and surveyed the hallway. Empty. On the plus side, that meant no sign of Sara's pitching phenom. On the negative, it meant no sign of Noelle, either.

Oh, well, he thought as he veered left toward his room. You had to take the good with the bad. Such was life.

The second his door latched behind him, he reached for the hem of his shirt. He had it half way up his torso when a flashing light on the nightstand caught his eye.

A message. On the room phone. The only people who even knew he was there were team management, his agent, his dad, Cooper and Reid, not necessarily in that order. Why hadn't they tried his cell?

Shit. He'd turned it off before his therapy session. Sara's number one rule. No phones. No interruptions.

He reached into the pocket of his gym shorts.

Nothing.

Double shit.

It must have slipped out during his workout. Hopefully someone had picked it up. He'd have to go back and get it, but not until he found out what was so important someone had tracked him down and left a message on his room phone.

He let his shirt fall and caught a whiff of sweat, reminding him that he'd better shower, too, before rejoining civilization.

But first the phone.

Jace sat down on his bed and hit the flashing button.

"Hey, pal," his father's voice greeted him over the speaker. "I tried your cell but it went straight to voice mail."

Duh.

"Anyway," his dad continued. "I, uh, need to talk to you. Nothing urgent, really. Just, uh, when you get a chance. Hope the arm's feeling better. Don't forget to ice it, and wear your brace even when you're sleeping."

The message ended, and Jace hit Delete. He loved his dad. How could he not? The guy had raised him solo when his mom ran off with a better prospect, one sure to make it to the show, not like his journeyman infielder father. But that didn't mean his dad wasn't downright annoying sometimes. Especially when it came to his favorite subject: baseball.

He stared at the phone a minute before picking up the handset and dialing his father's number, bracing himself for the questions to come, questions he didn't have any definitive answers to.

"Hi, Dad," Jace said when his father finally answered on the fourth ring. "Sorry I missed your call. I had my cell off during PT."

"How's it going?" His dad sounded out of breath, and not for the first time Jace wondered if he shouldn't be the one getting medical treatment.

"Good. My therapist says I'm ahead of schedule." Jace crossed the fingers of his good hand behind his back. "How about you? You sound tired."

"I'm fine. I ran in from the garage when I heard the phone."

"Working on something special?" Jace leaned back against his pillow, stretched his legs out on the bed and smiled, imagining his father tinkering with an old Crosley radio or vintage Pioneer television. It had been a hobby when his dad played ball, but when his career on the field had ended in Double-A he'd turned it into a viable business, repairing all kinds of small electronics, new and old. If it had wires, Patrick Monroe could fix it.

"A jukebox." His father's voice radiated excitement for his new project, even over the phone. "Wurlitzer, mid-1940s."

"That's gotta be rare." To Jace's knowledge, his father hadn't worked on one that old before. They'd restored a 1970s Seeburg together when Jace was in high school. "I can't wait to see it."

"Well, you'll have to. I don't want you rushing home on my account. Listen to your doctors and take your rehab one day at a time. Baseball's not going anywhere. It'll still be there when you're ready to play. And the team needs you at full strength."

Oh, goodie. Lecture time.

"I know, Dad. I'll be a model patient and follow doctor's orders to the letter. Promise." Good thing his fingers

were still crossed. "Now what was it you needed to talk to me about? You said in your message it wasn't urgent, but it must be pretty important if it couldn't wait until our Sunday call."

It was a ritual, the Sunday call, one they'd never missed in the ten years since Jace was drafted into the minors straight out of high school. 6:00 p.m. on the button unless Jace was on the field or in the air, and then he'd call as soon as the game was over or he touched down.

"It's nothing, really."

"C'mon, Dad. Whatever it is, it's not nothing or you wouldn't have called." Jace sat up and swung his feet over the side of the bed. "Are you hurt? Sick? Do you need me to come home?"

"No, no and no," his father insisted. "I told you, I don't want you cutting your rehab short for me. I'm just a little low on cash is all."

Again? Jace wanted to scream. But this was his father, the man who'd made sure he was fed and clothed and got to school on time, who'd scrimped and saved so his son could attend baseball camp every summer. And Jace had more than enough disposable income. Who was he to deny his own flesh and blood?

"How low?" he asked.

"Well, the basement's leaking and the refrigerator is on its last legs…"

Already? He'd bought a practically brand-new house for his dad eight years ago when he was called up to the majors.

"How low?" Jace repeated.

There was a long pause before his father answered, and when he did his voice was barely a whisper. "Ten grand."

"For a leak and a fridge?" Jace spat out before he could stop himself.

"The leak's pretty bad. The whole basement's underwater when it rains. They want to install a drainage system and a sump pump."

"They?"

"The waterproofing company."

Jace sighed and ran a hand through his hair. "How soon do you need the cash?"

"As soon as you can get it to me. The contractors want to start before the next big rain."

Jace glanced at the clock on the nightstand. 3:00 p.m. Still plenty of time to call the bank before it closed. "Okay. I'll have the money transferred into your account this afternoon."

"Thanks, son. You're a lifesaver."

"Love you, Dad. Talk to you Sunday."

Jace ended the call and tossed the phone onto the bed next to him. He'd get to the bank in a few minutes.

But first he was taking that damn shower.

NOELLE CRACKED THE door of the physical therapy room open and peeked inside.

All clear. No Jace. It was crazy to hide from him like a scared rabbit. Her luck was bound to run out sooner or later. But she'd rather it be later. Much later.

With a sigh of relief, she pushed the door open the rest of the way and limped inside.

"Noelle." Sara waved her over almost before she'd crossed the threshold. "Come meet our newest patient."

A boy who looked to be in his late teens sat on an exercise mat next to the kneeling Sara. One of his arms was missing below the elbow, the stump wrapped in a compression bandage.

"This is Dylan," Sara continued, sitting cross-legged in front of him and connecting a resistance band to a strap around his bicep. "We're getting him ready for his prosthetic."

Dylan looked up at Noelle through long, sandy bangs. "I'd shake your hand, but I've only got one and it's occupied at the moment."

"What have I told you about the amputee jokes?" Sara handed him the other end of the resistance band.

"The more the merrier?" Dylan suggested with a sarcastic grin.

"More like one is one too many," Sara countered.

Dylan rolled his eyes. "Hey, I might have lost my arm, but I haven't lost my sense of humor."

"Good thing." Noelle smiled in spite of herself. She liked this cocky kid. "You're gonna need it in this place."

"Everyone's a comedian." Sara shook her head. "Dylan, this is Noelle. She's an athlete, too."

"Oh, yeah?" He brushed his bangs out of his eyes to study her. "What's your sport?"

"Ballet." She watched for some sign of disdain, but instead, he nodded and continued to stare at her, his expression serious. "What's yours?"

"Baseball." His gaze shifted to his injured arm. "At least it was."

"Baseball?" Noelle caught Sara's eye, at once acutely aware of who Dylan reminded her of. "Has he met…?"

"Not yet," Sara said, cutting her off with a warning glare. "But soon. I hope."

"Met who?" Dylan asked.

"Never you mind. It's a surprise for when you're on your best behavior." Sara stood and motioned for him to do the same. "Enough chit-chat. You've got your re-

sistance bands, and you know how to use them. Get to work."

"Aye, aye, captain." He marched off toward the far corner of the room, where the cable and pulley machines were located.

"That's what I like to hear." Sara turned her attention to Noelle. "Let's get you started on the stationary bike. Same speed as yesterday, but you can up the distance an extra half mile. Then we'll do some range-of-motion exercises."

"Sure." Noelle pressed her lips together, trying to hide her disappointment. She'd been on the damn bike for a week. She was hoping to graduate to something a little more challenging, like maybe the elliptical or even the treadmill. Oh, well. Like Little Orphan Annie said—or sang—there was always tomorrow.

She started for the row of bikes but stopped when she saw a flash of silver under one of the benches. She bent and picked up a cell phone.

"I think someone dropped this," she said, holding it up.

"Where did you find it?" Sara asked.

"Under that bench," Noelle answered, pointing.

"Jace was there last. It must be his." Sara looked around the busy room and frowned. "I hate to ask, but could you bring it to him?"

Noelle flipped the phone over. Any hope she had that Sara was wrong was dashed by the sticker on the back of the case. Thor, complete with lightning bolt and baseball bat.

The Storm logo.

Of all the patients in this joint, why did it have to be his?

"Now?" she asked.

"If I know Jace, he's already hunting for it. He said he had some calls to make."

Noelle swallowed hard, searching for an excuse—any excuse—to say no. She didn't even care how ungracious she sounded. "What about my PT session?"

Sara consulted a chart on the wall. "Come back in an hour. I'll squeeze you in then."

"Isn't there anyone else who can do it?" Christ, she sounded like a whiny five-year-old.

Sara waved an arm, gesturing around the room. "Everyone else is otherwise occupied. Besides, you know where his room is."

"I…I do?" Noelle stammered. "I mean, I do, but how do you…?"

"He told me you took my advice and apologized for listening in on us and thinking the worst."

"Oh."

"Yeah, oh." Sara squinted at her. "You're holding out on me."

"I don't know what you mean." Noelle wiped her suddenly clammy palms on her shorts.

"Yes, you do." Sara put her hands on her hips. "Something's going on with you and Jace."

"What… ?" Noelle lowered her voice. "What would make you think that?"

"First, you all but refuse to bring him his phone. Then you get squirrelly about being in his room. Seems pretty suspicious to me."

"Well, it's not." Noelle stamped her good foot for emphasis. "There's absolutely nothing going on between us. I barely know the man."

"Good. Then it won't be a problem for you to give him his phone."

Trapped.

"Of course not," Noelle said with forced lightness. "I'll see you in sixty."

Woman up, she told herself as she limped out the door and down the hall. *You got this. Just knock on his door, hand him his phone and go. No smiles. No small talk. And definitely no steamy kisses.*

The first part of her plan was no problem. She made her way to his room and knocked. And knocked. And knocked. She even tried calling out his name.

No answer. Too bad the darned phone wasn't thin enough to slip under the door.

In a last-ditch move, she tried the knob. If she was lucky, she could leave the phone just inside the door and slip away unnoticed.

She was lucky.

The knob turned and she inched the door open. The sound of running water greeted her, explaining why Jace hadn't answered the door.

He was in the shower.

Which, of course, conjured all sorts of X-rated images in her head. Like Jace naked. And wet. And best— or worst—of all, hard. Every naked, wet inch of him.

Noelle shook her head to clear her thoughts—fat lot of good that did—and stepped gingerly into the room. She was all set to drop off the phone and hightail it out of there as fast as she could with one good leg when she heard a thud, then a moan, from the bathroom.

"Jace?" She froze, the phone still in her hand. "Are you okay?"

Another moan, this one longer, more guttural, almost a growl.

She put the phone down on the nightstand and pressed her ear to the bathroom door. "Jace?"

Still no response.

Damn.

How did she get herself into these predicaments?

He was probably fine. Doing what guys did in the shower when they were horny or bored or whatever. She'd done what she promised, brought him his stupid phone. And now she could—should—leave.

But what if he wasn't okay?

Double damn.

She eased the door open, telling herself her motives were noble, not naughty. She'd only look long enough to make sure he wasn't crumpled in a heap at the bottom of the bathtub. And if she happened to get a glimpse of a bulging bicep or slick pec or—heaven forbid—stiff cock, she'd just look down and back away quickly.

Very quickly.

5

JACE LEANED AGAINST the smooth, cool tile, letting the warm water pound his chest as he jerked himself into oblivion. He rolled his thumb over the head of his cock, imagining how the Duchess would react if she could see him now. And how he'd like her to react.

She had a perfect mouth, red, ripe and lush. He hadn't stopped thinking about it since their kiss. If he had his way, she'd be on her knees now with it wrapped around him. He closed his eyes and pictured her lips closing around his crown, her tongue stealing out to capture the drops of pre-come gathered at the slit.

His balls tightened and he squeezed his cock as he slid his soapy hand up and down the soft skin. He was close, so damn close.

But not yet.

He slowed his movements, not wanting the movie playing in his mind to end. Now Noelle was rising, sliding her slick body up his, thigh meeting thigh, breast meeting chest. Her pale skin glowed against his perpetual California tan. In his mind, she was perfectly smooth everywhere, and when she lifted one leg to hook it around

his waist her sleek, bare pussy brushed against the tip of
his rock-hard dick.

With a groan, Jace thrust into his fist, his need to come
trumping his desire to prolong the sweet torture of his
dirty daydream. He imagined he was driving into Noelle,
pounding her, hammering her, her wet heat clenching
around him until she was as desperate as him for release.

His thighs shook as he moved his good hand faster and
faster over his straining cock. His hips moved in rhythm
with his fist and his chest heaved, his lungs struggling
to draw air as he climbed closer to climax.

It hit him like a runner sliding into second, hard and
fast. He swore and called out her name as he came, hitting the wall and floor of the shower, the last burst land-
ing hot on his chest. He slumped against the cold tile, his
fist still gripped around his throbbing cock.

Fuck. If just fantasizing about doing it with Noelle
was that explosive, he was afraid to think what might
happen if they actually had sex.

He turned the water temperature down a notch, figuring a splash of cold was just the thing to snap him
back to reality. He'd barely started to lather up when a
crash, followed by a high-pitched, distinctly female "shit"
stopped him cold.

"Who's there?" he barked, hastily rinsing himself before shutting off the water.

The only answer was the snick of metal against metal
as the door caught in the latch.

Someone was there. Or had been. Listening to—or
even watching—him.

And not just someone. A female someone.

*Noelle? Had she seen him? Heard him cry out her
name as he came?*

He grabbed a towel off the rack, patted himself dry

and had it fastened around his waist before you could say "ground rule double." But when he opened the bathroom door, his room was empty.

He scanned from corner to corner, searching for some clue as to who had been there. Whatever his visitor had crashed into was apparently still intact and had been put back in its proper place. But his eyes stopped on one familiar object that definitely wasn't there when he went to shower.

His cell phone. The one he'd lost in PT. On the table next to his bed.

So his voyeur was also a Good Samaritan. That explained what she'd been doing there in the first place. But it didn't leave him any closer to knowing her identity.

Yet.

He picked up the phone and turned it on, thanking his lucky stars Sara had insisted they exchange cell numbers. Ignoring the notifications that flashed on the screen, he opened a new text message and started typing.

Thanks for dropping off my phone. Hope you enjoyed the show.

He figured he'd have to wait for her response after he hit Send, but he was wrong. She must have been between patients or on a break or something, because almost immediately he could see she'd started typing. A few seconds later, her answer appeared.

Not me, hot shot. You can thank your ballerina friend. Can't wait to hear about the show.

She ended the text with a winky face emoji.

Jackpot. Noelle was his Peeping Tom. Again. And

this time she'd gotten even more of an eyeful—and ear-ful—than last time.

Whistling, he texted Sara back.

I'd do that if I could find her. Haven't seen her all week.

He hoped Sara might have some idea of Noelle's whereabouts. Then he could ambush the Duchess and have some fun messing with her.

And man, did he want to mess with her. Big time.

Again, Sara's answer came quickly.

She'll be here any minute. Has PT until 4:00. And you know my zero tolerance policy on interruptions.

Jace checked the clock on his phone. He had just enough time to change, return a few calls, and be lying in wait for Noelle outside the PT room when she finished up with Sara. His thumbs flew on the keyboard as he sent his response.

No problem. Tell her I'll catch up with her at dinner. Thx.

Satisfied with his crack diversionary tactic, Jace tossed the phone onto the bed and crossed to the closet, where he pulled out a pair of well-worn jeans and a plain, white T-shirt. The corners of his mouth curved into a knowing smile as he dropped his towel and started to get dressed.

4:00 p.m. Game time. Then Noelle would see what happened to bad girls who liked to spy on poor, unsuspecting, naked men.

And hopefully by the end of the night they'd *both* wind up naked. And satisfied.

"ARE YOU SURE you're okay?" Sara handed Noelle a water bottle. "You're not your normal, take-no-prisoners self today. You seem—I don't know—distracted."

Duh. Watching the hottest guy on either side of the Mississippi get himself off would do that to a girl. Not that she was admitting that to Sara.

"For the hundredth time, I'm fine." Noelle popped the top on the bottle and took a sip before carefully climbing off the recumbent bike. "Now can we get to the range-of-motion exercises, or what?"

The more activity, the better. Maybe working herself past the point of exhaustion would help erase the image of Jace all naked and wet and hard, calling out her name as he came.

Not likely.

"In a minute." Sara took a seat on one of the weight benches and motioned for Noelle to join her. "Take a breather. Have some more water."

With a resigned shrug, Noelle complied, sitting and drinking. The water was cool and refreshing and totally ineffective in dampening her runaway libido.

"What now?" she asked when she'd finished. "Girl bonding time?"

"In a manner of speaking." Sara sipped from her own water bottle. "So you and Jace…"

"I told you, there is no me and Jace."

"That's not what I heard."

Noelle could almost feel her pale skin blanch even further. "Heard? From who?"

"The man himself. He texted to thank me for returning his phone."

Oh shit, oh shit, oh shit, oh shit, oh shit.

"What did you say?"

"I set him straight. Told him it was you."

Great. Now he knew she'd been spying on him. Again.

"He said you got quite a show." Sara snickered.

"He told you about that?" Noelle squeaked.

Gentlemen were not supposed to tattle. Of course, ladies weren't supposed to snoop, either.

"Not in detail." Sara eyed Noelle hopefully.

"Well, you're not getting anything out of me." Noelle pushed her shoulders back and lifted her chin.

"What happened?" Sara persisted, undaunted. "Did you walk in on him in the buff?"

It was amazing how close she'd come to hitting the nail on the head. So to speak.

"I plead the fifth," Noelle said, trotting out a phrase her lawyer brother loved to use.

"Interesting." Sara narrowed her eyes. "People who refuse to talk usually have something to hide."

"Not this people." Noelle took a long slug from her water bottle and stood. "Now if the Spanish Inquisition is over, can I pretty please get back to my workout? There's an eighteen-year-old soloist in the company who'd give her favorite pair of legwarmers to take my principal spot."

"We can't have that, can we?" Sara rose and picked out a five-pound ankle cuff from a shelf against the wall. "Start with hamstring curls. Three sets of twelve, rest, then repeat."

She handed Noelle the cuff and pointed in the direction of an empty mat. "But don't think this discussion is over. I have ways of making you talk."

"Over and above the daily physical torture?"

"You ain't seen nothin' yet." Sara promised, giving her a gentle shove. "I haven't even begun to torture you."

She wasn't kidding. Half an hour and what seemed like ten gallons of sweat later, Noelle lay drenched and

panting on the mat, having been put through more curls, lifts, bends, raises and squats than she could count.

"Ready to throw in the towel?" Sara taunted.

Yes! Noelle's leg screamed.

"No way," her mouth contradicted.

Sara checked the clock over the door. "Well, my next victim should be here any time now, so you're off the hook. Go take a nice, hot shower. You worked hard. You deserve it."

"Thanks." Noelle ducked her head and made a beeline for the door so Sara wouldn't see her blush at the word "shower." Would she ever hear that word again without seeing Jace braced against the wall, his hand a blur as he stroked himself, his eyes closed and his head thrown back in ecstasy?

Her head was still down when she plowed through the door and ran smack into a broad, male—very familiar—chest.

"Hey there, Duchess." Jace closed his fingers over her shoulders, catching her before she knocked them both over. "What's your hurry?"

She shivered, his touch burning through the thin fabric of her tank top and sending waves of need low in her belly. "I wish you'd stop calling me that."

"I'll make you a deal." He favored her with that panty-melting, bad-boy smile that made her common sense do a grand jeté out the window. "I'll stop calling you Duchess if you quit the Peeping Tom stuff."

She tensed, knowing he had her dead to rights. Still, denial seemed like the best defense. "I don't know what you're talking about."

"Don't you?" He leaned in, his hot breath fanning the hair at the nape of her neck as he spoke. "You know, if you wanted to see me naked, all you had to do was ask."

She jerked back. "I do not want to see you naked."

"Again." His fingers tightened around her arms. "You don't want to see me naked again. Except your body says otherwise."

"My body?"

"The flushed cheeks. Parted lips. Nipples as hard as bullets." He bent impossibly closer so his lips brushed her ear. "They don't lie, sweetness."

She bit back her sharp retort when the door to the PT room bust open and Dylan came out.

"Dylan." She shrank away from Jace. At least this time he had the courtesy to let her go. "I thought you left."

"I did." The teenager held up an iPod. "I came back for this. You were busy with Sara."

His eyes moved to Jace, and the shock of recognition crossed his youthful face. "Holy crap. You're Jace Monroe."

"I'm aware of that." Jace rocked back on his heels, an amused chuckle softening his words.

"You hit for the cycle in the All-Star game."

"I'm aware of that, too."

"You were on pace to break Barry Bonds's single-season home run record." Dylan eyed the shortstop's brace. "I read about your injury. Tough break."

"You, too." Jace's eyes flicked to the boy's missing arm. "Sara says you're quite a pitcher."

"Was," Dylan muttered, scuffing the linoleum with the toe of his cross-trainers.

"Ever hear of Jim Abbott?" Jace asked.

Dylan shook his head.

"Pete Gray?"

Another head shake, sandy hair flopping in every direction.

"Tell you what." Jace clapped a hand on Dylan's good

shoulder. "Meet me tomorrow morning for breakfast and we can talk. Dining room, eight a.m. sharp."

He offered his hand—his injured right one, Noelle noticed, so Dylan, who was missing his left, wouldn't feel awkward. Dylan took it carefully and shook it.

"Sure thing, Mr. Monroe."

"My friends call me Jace."

"You bet, Mr....Jace." Dylan practically bounced down the hall, his words floating after him. "See you at eight."

Smiling, Noelle watched him go, grateful not just for the boy's obvious delight but for his interruption, which had burst the bubble of sexual tension surrounding her and Jace.

"Another loyal fan?" she teased.

Jace shrugged. "Kid probably knows my stats better than I do."

"You must get that a lot." She leaned against the wall, her knee starting to feel the strain of standing for so long after her workout.

He shrugged again. "I could say the same to you."

She reached up and took out her ponytail, shaking her hair free. God, that felt good. "Ballet fans aren't quite so...enthusiastic. And I usually don't offer to have breakfast with them."

"Neither do I," Jace's voice sounded strained, and he stopped to clear his throat. "But the kid's at a crossroads. How he deals with the next few weeks of rehab will determine whether he ever sets foot on the mound again."

"You mean he could still pitch?" she asked.

"With the right prosthetic and a shit-ton of guts, sure."

"And Jim Abbott and Pete Gray—whoever they are—can help him?"

"Maybe."

She stared at Jace. The tattoos. The five-o'clock shadow. The cocky attitude.

She jabbed a finger at his chest. "And to think you had me fooled."

He quirked a brow at her. "How so?"

"Under that tough-guy exterior, you're just a big, old marshmallow with a heart of gold, aren't you?"

"Because I'm having breakfast with a fan?"

"Because you reached out to a scared kid facing an uncertain future."

Like we are.

He stuffed his hands in his pockets. "Whatever you say, Duchess. I'm a regular Mother Teresa. Just don't tell the tabloids. I have a reputation to uphold."

So much for Mr. Nice Guy. "I thought you agreed to stop calling me that."

Noelle pushed off the wall and headed for her room.

"Only if you stop stalking me," Jace said, following her. "And I haven't seen any evidence of that yet."

"I am not stalking you." In fact, at the moment it seemed an awful lot like he was stalking her. But she didn't think it was wise to bring that up since she *was* guilty of the whole Peeping Tom thing.

"What else do you call breaking into my room and…"

"Stop." The word came out on a shriek so loud a geriatric patient going past them almost lost his grip on his walker. Noelle mumbled an apology and rounded the corner at the end of the hall, picking up the pace as best as she could with her bum knee. When she spoke again, it was practically a hiss. "I did not break into your room. And I did not spy on you. I returned your phone. I left."

Eventually.

"Eventually," he quipped, echoing her thoughts. What was he, a mind reader?

Thankfully, they'd reached her door. The peace and quiet of her Jace-free room was mere inches away. All she had to do was get the dang thing open and get rid of him and his bedroom eyes and his sexy smile and his hotter-than-hot body. She fumbled for her key, finally pulling it out of her pocket and slipping it into the lock.

"Well, this has been fun." *Not.* "But it's time for this girl to soak her tired muscles in a warm bath."

Those damn bedroom eyes gleamed, and she cursed herself for giving him an opening as wide as the stage at the Palais Garnier. "Sure you don't want company? I could watch. Maybe even scrub your back if you ask nicely. After all, turnabout is fair play."

She pushed the door open, not bothering to deny—yet again—that she'd seen him. "Thanks, but no."

Once inside, she spun around to close the door. Instead, she found him looming over her, one hand hanging on the top of the door frame. "If you change your mind, you know where to find me."

His low, sexy drawl vibrated through her, making her wish that was an option. "Don't hold your breath."

"I won't." With his free hand, he brushed a stray lock of hair off her cheek, and the faint tremors his voice had started increased to near earthquake level. "Lock your door if you want any privacy. I hear this place has a problem with folks waltzing in to people's rooms at the most inopportune moments."

With a wink, he left.

6

DOOR FIRMLY LATCHED, Noelle eased herself down onto her bed, still trembling. Jace was like some sort of sexual Svengali, able to bring out all kinds of indecent, primal urges she'd suppressed since her breakup with Yannick. Like the urge to climb all over him as if he was her own personal jungle gym. She needed a few minutes for her traitorous body to recover.

She'd closed her eyes for maybe thirty seconds when her cell went off on the bedside table. Her screen told her it was Ivy, wanting to FaceTime. She sat up and ran a hand through her hair before answering.

"Well, if it isn't the elusive, world-famous fashion photographer. Back from—where was it this time?"

"Bondi Beach." Ivy unwrapped a Milky Way bar and bit into it. "And I'm not a fashion photographer anymore. I'm a simple, hometown shutterbug, taking pics of family and friends for fun and profit. This was a one-time favor."

Noelle's stomach grumbled. She hadn't had chocolate in, like, forever. The macaroons had been an aberration, her lone indulgence in as far back as she could remember. And she'd wound up leaving them on that bench, too shaken by a simple kiss to think of food.

Simple kiss, my ass.

"Andre still pestering you to come back?" she asked, trying to get her mind back on task.

"No. He knows I'm happy doing what I'm doing. But he was double-booked and Cade had a few days off coming to him, so…"

A wistful look drifted across her sister's face on the tiny screen, and Noelle could imagine how Ivy and her new hunk—who also happened to be their brother's best friend—had used their unexpected vacation time. Not that she particularly wanted to. First Holly, now Ivy. One sexually satisfied sister was bad enough. Two was almost unbearable. And that wasn't even counting her disgustingly happy third sibling and his fiancée. Love was spreading like wildfire in the Nelson family. Unless your name was Noelle.

She shook off the sudden feeling of melancholy.

"So it's true." Phone in hand, she walked to the minifridge in the cabinet under the television and pulled out a bottle of water. Staying hydrated was an important part of injury prevention and rehabilitation. And maybe filling up on H2O would kill her craving for chocolate. And sexy shortstops. "You really are giving it all up to stay in Stockton."

"I'm not giving. I'm gaining." Ivy took another, even bigger, bite of her candy bar. "Something you might consider someday—when the right guy comes along."

She sounded strangely like…

"Have you been talking to Holly?" Noelle sank into the stuffed chair by the window, stretching her leg out in front of her.

Ivy licked a spot of chocolate off her upper lip. "She is my sister."

"So am I."

"I know. That's why I'm worried about you."

"My knee's going to be fine. I'll be dancing again in no time."

"It's not your knee I'm worried about. Or your career."

"Then what?" Noelle cracked open the water bottle and took a long, satisfying slug. "And please don't say my heart."

That ship had sailed with Yannick. She'd given herself up to him, trusted him with not just her heart but her career. She'd even brought him home and introduced him to her family, something she almost never did with her "city boys," as her father dubbed them.

And how had the lowlife repaid her? By using her, building her up as his inspiration, choreographing ballets around her, only to replace her in his bed with a younger, fresher prospect in the corps with perkier tits, a tighter ass and fewer functioning brain cells. And to make bad matters even worse, he'd turned the whole thing into a public spectacle, ditching her on stage, in front of the entire company.

Later, one of the soloists had discretely pulled her aside and advised her to get tested. Seemed their esteemed choreographer had been dallying with his new muse for months. But somehow what was common knowledge among the company had escaped Noelle's not-so-keen observation.

She was negative, thank God. But it would be a long time—maybe even forever—before she let herself be that vulnerable again.

Ivy's voice brought Noelle back to the present. "Holly told me about your baseball player."

Figures.

"He is not my baseball player."

"She says he's a walking wet dream."

"Holly so did not say that."

"Okay, maybe the words were mine. But the sentiment was hers."

Now *that* Noelle believed. "What other sentiments did she share with you?"

"Just that you had some sort of misunderstanding and owed him an apology." Ivy popped the last of the candy in her mouth, balled up the wrapper and tossed it off screen. "How did it go? Did you kiss and make up?"

Yes and no.

Ivy's eyes widened. "So, yes to the kiss and no to the making up?"

Damn. She hadn't meant to say that out loud. Noelle considered backpedaling, but she'd never been very good at lying, as Holly had so aptly pointed out the last time they'd talked. So this time she opted for a partial dose of honesty. "Okay, so we kissed. It was no big deal."

"No big deal?" Ivy squealed. "He's the first guy you've given the time of day since that douchebag Yakov."

"Yannick."

"Whatever." Ivy's face disappeared from the screen for a split second. When she returned, her image was blurry. "The important part is you kissed him. That's a huge step."

"He kissed me. And you're holding the phone too close. You look like a giant, fuzzy redheaded caterpillar."

"Gee, thanks." Ivy's face came back into focus. "Better?"

"Much."

"Now back to that kiss…"

Noelle sighed and took another drink, stalling for time. "Can't we talk about something else? Like *your* love life? Or global thermonuclear war?"

Hell, even the state of the world economy would be a

better, or at least easier, topic for discussion than her relationship—for lack of a better word—with Jace.

"Negative." Ivy shook her head, sending her auburn
curls into a riot. "I'm under strict instructions not to hang
up until I get the whole scoop on you and Mr. MVP."

"Let me guess." Not that it required much deduction.
The nickname was a dead giveaway. "Our beloved big
sister give you marching orders?"

"Yep. I can't wait to tell her you actually tongue-
wrestled the guy. Does he kiss as good as he looks?"

Tongue-wrestled? Ivy had been hanging out with Cade
and his firefighter buddies too long.

"Who said anything about tongues? And how do you
even know what he looks like?"

Ivy touched a finger to her cheek and rolled her eyes
upward. "Google is a beautiful thing. And so is Jace
Monroe. Any man who looks like that definitely knows
how to use his tongue."

Noelle didn't even try to argue. "He caught me in a
moment of weakness. But it's not going to happen again."

"Why in the name of all that's holy not?" Ivy shrieked.

In the background Noelle heard a plaintive meow.
Her sister bent, moving out of frame. When she reap-
peared, she held a grumpy-looking tabby cat. "Sorry,
Piper. Didn't mean to disturb your nap."

"Look, just because you and Holly are blissfully mated
doesn't mean I'm going there."

"Blissfully mated?" Ivy scoffed, kissing the cat on the
nose and setting him down.

"You know what I mean."

"Yeah," Ivy said, her voice taking on a dream-like
quality. "I do. But no one said anything about you falling
in love. It's been six months since He-Who-Shall-Not-

Be-Named showed his true colors. You're way overdue for a rebound guy."

"I'm not sure I can do the rebound thing." Noelle finished off her water and set the empty bottle down on the floor next to her chair. "How do you get involved without, you know, getting involved?"

"Beats me." Ivy laughed. "I thought Cade and I were just a fling. And look how that turned out. Not that I'm complaining."

"That's what I'm afraid of," Noelle muttered. Not softly enough, apparently.

"There's your problem right there." Ivy pointed her finger at the screen. "Fear."

"You're telling me you weren't scared when you started your—what did you call it?—fling with Cade?"

"You bet your ass I was." Ivy laughed again, prompting another meow from the once again invisible Piper. "But I didn't let it stop me. And neither should you. At a minimum, you'll get good and laid. Let off some sexual tension so you can focus on your rehab."

Her sister had a point there. Even Sara had noticed. It had been impossible for Noelle to concentrate on anything but Jace and his lethal weapon lips since that damn kiss. Some hot and heavy action between the sheets— or against the wall or on the bathroom counter—might be just the ticket to get him out of her system, lips and all. Then her rehab would be front and center again, no distractions.

"Aha!" Ivy aimed another accusing finger at her. "I'm right, and you know I am. Stop thinking about it and just do it already."

"Maybe I will, and maybe I won't." Noelle tried to sound nonchalant, but her heart rate climbed to near NASCAR speed at the thought of full-body contact with

Jace. "Right now I've got more pressing matters to attend to. Like showering. And sleeping."

Ivy stuck her tongue out and blew out a raspberry. "How is that more pressing than sex?"

"It is when one, you stink so bad no man would get within ten feet of you, and two, even if by some miracle one did you'd be too exhausted to do anything about it."

"Okay, you win that round." Ivy wrinkled her nose. "Come to think of it, Cade's shift ends in half an hour and I'm pretty rank. Photographing a five-year-old's birthday party outdoors at high noon in the first full week of summer will do that to you."

"Looks like I'm not the only one headed for the shower." Noelle smiled.

Ivy eyes took on a mischievous glint and she licked her lips. "Then again, some of our best sex has been when we're both sweaty, hot and bothered. I think it turns him on. One time…"

"Stop, I beg of you. Stop." Noelle's smile turned to a grimace. "What is it with you and Holly and the incessant TMI?"

Ivy lifted one shoulder, and her voice got all dreamy again. "I guess when you're happy, you want to share that happiness with the people you love. Someday you'll understand. Maybe sooner than you think."

Before Noelle could get the "don't bet on it" that was bouncing around her head to come out of her mouth, her sister was signing off. "Gotta run. Don't wait too long to start Operation Boink The Ballplayer. And let me know how it goes."

There is no Operation Boink The Ballplayer, Noelle thought as she ended the call and clumped into the bathroom. She turned on the water, adjusted the temperature as high as it would go and sat on the toilet to watch the

tub fill. She'd told Jace she was going to soak in a long, hot bath, and that's what she aimed to do. Hopefully, it would be more relaxing than a quick shower.

And less likely to remind her of a certain shortstop and his seven plus inches of hardwood.

HE ALMOST MISSED the soft knock at the door.

Jace was in bed, eyes closed, in that misty, magical place between awake and asleep. The place where No-elle Nelson danced through his half dreams. But this ballerina was no sugarplum fairy, she was a fair-haired femme fatale, tempting him with her sultry eyes and her bee-stung lips and her long dancer's legs.

Then the knock had brought him fully awake and he'd swung his door open to find the temptress standing right in front of him.

He rubbed his tired eyes to make sure he wasn't hallucinating.

Nope. She was there, eyes, lips, legs and all.

"Another late-night visit?" He yawned and scratched his bare chest, getting a perverse sense of satisfaction when her gaze followed his hand over his pecs down the trail of hair that bisected his abs and disappeared under the waistband of his sweats. "To what do I owe the pleasure?"

"So it's a pleasure. That's a start." She glanced up and down the hall, her ash-blond hair, still mussed, he presumed, from sleep, swinging gently. "Can I come in?"

"Sure, since you asked so nicely." He stepped back to let her pass. "This time."

She spun around, her eyes shooting poisoned darts at him. "What happened this afternoon was…"

"Stop." He held up his hands in a gesture of surrender. "I don't want to fight."

She loosened her clenched fists and let out a long, slow sigh, like his words had deflated her anger. "Neither do I. But that's what we seem to do."

"Any idea how we can change that?" Because he had a few. Most of which involved him and her and a conspicuous absence of clothing. In his experience, it was hard to fight when you were skin to skin.

"That's sort of why I'm here." She twisted the hem of her shirt. "Mind if I sit?"

"Yes, I do." He advanced on her, backing her up against the bed. "I don't think you came to sit. Or to talk."

"No?" Her voice was breathy and she stared down at her hands, which had wrung her shirt into a knot.

"No." He slid a finger under her chin, tipping it up and forcing her eyes to meet his. Desire and doubt swirled in their indigo depths. The first he approved wholeheartedly, but the second had to go. "I think you came to finish what we started on that bench. In private. Without the cookies, unfortunately."

"What makes you think that?"

He knew what she was getting at but decided to play dumb and go for the laugh, hoping it would loosen her up. "Well, for one thing, your hands are empty, unless you count that shirt you're destroying. And I doubt you're hiding a tin of cookies in your bra."

It worked. Her shoulders relaxed and she let the hem of her shirt fall. "Not the cookies. The finishing what we started."

"I told you, your body doesn't lie." He wedged a leg between hers, pressing against her core. "And neither does mine."

"Wow. That's a pretty impressive, um, truth, you've got there."

"You ain't seen nothin' yet, Duchess." But she would, if he had anything to say about it. And soon.

He laughed softly, brushing his mouth across her temple, and she shivered. "I thought I told you not to call me that."

"You did." He brought his arms around her waist, pulling her even tighter to him. "But I know down deep you like it."

"Maybe way down deep." Her hands crept up between them, coming to rest on his chest, her palms cold on his superheated skin. "So we're really going to do this?"

He sucked in a breath as her fingers tangled in his chest hair. "Is that a statement or a question?"

"A question."

"My vote's yes." He lowered his head for a kiss, his lips grazing hers just long enough to tease. "But it has to be unanimous."

He kissed her again, longer this time, deeper. When he came up for air, she wasn't the only one who was all hot and bothered, as evidenced by the giant tent in his pants. If she voted no, he was staring down the barrel at another long night alone, just him, his hand and the shower.

Unless she wanted to watch again…

He touched a finger to the hollow of her throat, where her pulse was going crazy. "What's it gonna be, sweetness?"

"This is a bad idea." She abandoned his chest hair for the hair at the nape of his neck, her actions warring with her words.

"Maybe." He gave her his most seductive smile, one that promised a world of wicked wonders. "But sometimes bad ideas are the best ones."

She waited so long to respond he lowered his hands

to his sides and started to back away. She stopped him with a hand on his forearm.

"Wait." She rubbed her lips together, and the tent in his pants went from teepee to circus. "I don't want you to go."

He stared down at the hand on his arm. Pale, delicate, her pink-tipped fingers trembling with nervous excitement. Or maybe it was fear. She was out of her comfort zone, that was for sure. Hell, so was he. Not that he cared.

"Don't worry," he reassured her, covering her hand with his own. "I'm not going far."

"You're not?"

She blinked, her long lashes sweeping her cheeks. Damn, her eyes were hypnotizing.

"Hell, no." He chuckled. "This is my room."

"Oh. Right." Her cheeks flushed with red but those hypnotic eyes never left his. "Well, I don't want to go, either."

"Then what do you want, Duchess?"

"You." She stepped closer to him, moving between his thighs. "I want you."

Reluctantly, he released her, but only to cross the room and lock the door. "Last chance to back out."

She lifted her chin. "I'm not backing out."

"You sure?" He crossed back to her, letting his hands rest on her shoulders, barely covered by the thin straps of her tank top. Was her skin that soft everywhere? "I'm not a one-and-done kind of guy. We're talking a whole night of debauchery here. You on top of me. Me on top of you. And any other position I can interest you in."

She glanced at his injured arm, not in the brace now since he'd been sleeping but still tender, his tattoos—and the scars from his surgery—clearly visible. "What about your arm? And my leg?"

"We'll just have to get creative. I'm well versed in

the Kama Sutra." Thanks to Reid and Cooper, who'd included a copy in his care package. It beat the heck out of anything on the shelves in Spaulding's pathetic excuse for a library. "Any other objections?"

He watched, transfixed, as she took a step back and reached for the hem of her shirt. This time, instead of balling it in her fists, she lifted it so slowly and deliberately he thought his cock was going to explode. Inch by creamy inch, she revealed her flat stomach and toned abs until the shirt was over her head and on the floor, leaving her in yoga pants that hugged her hips and a lacy lavender bra that didn't leave a whole hell of a lot to the imagination.

"Does that answer your question?"

7

TOM PETTY WAS RIGHT.

Waiting was the hardest part.

Like right now, as Noelle stood half naked in Jace's room, most of her breasts and all of her intentions bared to him, waiting for him to goddamn do—or say—something. Anything. Hell, at this point she'd take him picking up her shirt and throwing it at her. At least then she'd know what was going on in that all-too-handsome head of his.

She started to reach for it herself, convinced he'd changed his mind about the whole thing, when his deep, rough whisper stopped her.

"Don't. I was enjoying the view."

She straightened. "I thought…"

"Don't do that, either." He folded his arms across his impressive chest.

"Then what should I do?"

One corner of his mouth lifted. "First time at the rodeo?"

"Hardly." She blew a hair off her face. "Let's just say I'm not used to being the aggressor."

"Oh, so that's how you want to play it. Fine by me."

In two strides, he was at the bed. Without warning, he flopped onto it and stretched out, crossing his arms behind his head. "Here I am, sweetness. All yours. Just do what comes naturally and promise you'll still respect me in the morning."

"Still?" She matched his half smile with one of her own. "Wouldn't that imply I already respect you?"

"Good point. Forget about the respect and have your wicked way with me."

He crossed his ankles and wiggled his toes at her. Damn, even the man's bare feet were sexy. A far cry from hers, toes constantly bruised, bleeding and bandaged from dancing on pointe.

She shook her head to jar her rambling thoughts loose. *Idiot.* He'd just offered her free rein over his entire body, and there she was mooning over his feet. What a waste, when there were so many more interesting parts to explore.

And like her mother always said, *Waste not, want not.*

Of course, she also said act in haste, repent at leisure.

Shaking that thought away, too, Noelle toed off her ballet flats and slipped out of her yoga pants.

Jace's whiskey eyes darkened from a warm, medium brown to the color of dark, rich chocolate as they raked her nearly naked body from head to toe. "That's a look."

Noelle followed his gaze to her lacy, lilac bra, past the matching panties and down, down…to her bulky, black knee brace.

Talk about a buzz kill.

"Take it off," he ordered in the same deep, gravelly whisper he'd used to stop her from putting her shirt back on.

Oh, the irony.

She put her hands on her hips and tilted her head to study him. "I thought I was in charge."

"You are." His eyes latched onto hers and wouldn't let go. "As soon as you take it off."

"All of it?"

"Just the brace. Leave the rest for me."

She bent to loosen the Velcro straps.

Yep. Jace Monroe was a certified sexual Svengali. Why else would she be obeying his every command?

"Now you," she said once she had the brace off.

"Me what?" he asked innocently.

"Strip to your skivvies, superstar."

He plucked at the drawstring of his sweats. "These are my pajamas. I'm not wearing anything underneath."

"Even better."

"How about you give me a hand." He crooked a finger, beckoning her nearer. "After all, I am injured."

She walked toward him in almost a trance, drawn to him like metal to a magnet. "Sure, play that card."

"Whatever it takes to get your hands on me."

He patted the bed next to him and she sat, one hand instinctively drifting to the waistband of his sweat pants. He lifted his hips and she peeled them off, like she was unwrapping the best Christmas present ever.

A hard, hugely erect present she couldn't wait to touch and taste.

So she didn't.

"Damn, girl." Jace hissed as she bent to touch her tongue to his crown, circling it. "When you get down to it, you don't mess around. I like a woman who skips the appetizer and goes right for dessert."

She would have responded but by then she had him in her mouth, his musky smell and sweet, salty taste filling her senses.

"Oh, God." He groaned and twisted beneath her, and she stretched out beside him and sank down further, her tongue teasing the underside of his shaft as she closed her lips around him. With one hand, she gripped the base while the other traced the vee that ran from his hip to his groin.

His moans encouraged her to go faster, deeper, until he was almost at the back of her throat. No small feat given the size of his erection. And not something she was normally into. But it was like a dam inside her had burst, and now that she'd broken her six-month, self-imposed sexual drought there was no turning back.

She wanted it all. She wanted it now. Fierce and fast, slow and sweet, decadent and dangerous. Jace was hers for the night, and she intended to make the most of it.

Of him.

He groaned again and thrust into her mouth. His hands fisted in the sheets, and she looked up to find his eyes closed, his jaw tight. She smiled around him, struck by the realization that he was holding onto his self-control by a gossamer thread—and the feeling of power that came from knowing she'd brought him to that point.

She hummed against his skin, wanting to push him over the edge, and he pulsed against her tongue. Tension spiraled through her belly, winding its way down to her sex and making her clit tingle. If she so much as touched herself, she'd go off like a bottle rocket. But as much as she wanted to come, she wanted to make him come more.

She eased off, giving him teasing licks instead of the deep-throated suction she knew he wanted. She tortured him until his hands left the blanket and curled around her shoulders, drawing her almost imperceptibly closer. Then she went down on him with renewed gusto, suck-

ing hard and fast, savoring the sensation of his cock sliding in and out of her mouth.

"Stop," he growled, trying to pull away. "I'm going to come."

She released him with a pop but the hand at the base of his shaft kept him from going anywhere. "That's the plan."

"What about you?" He gazed down at her through heavy-lidded eyes, and she imagined how she might look to him, her hair splayed across his thigh, her lips swollen and wet with his juices.

"I thought you said we had all night."

"We do."

"Then lie back and let me take care of you." She angled his cock toward her mouth, her tongue stealing out to lick the tip. "And don't worry. I'll get my turn."

Damn straight she would.

Jace might be a bed-hopping bastard, but he wasn't a complete cad, certainly not one who put his own gratification over his partner's. Sex was supposed to be a mutual thing, not a one-way street. If he was going to come, Noelle was going to come right along with him.

Then they could start all over again.

"Slide on up here."

"Kind of busy at the moment." She licked him from stem to stern like he was an ice cream cone on a hot summer day and she was afraid he was going to melt away before she could finish. He let out a sort of strangled gasp and lifted his hips, arching into her.

"The busy end's not the end I'm interested in." He eyed the perfect globes of her perfect ass, lovingly cupped by her purple panties. "I was thinking we could make this a banquet for two."

"A what?" Her blue-green eyes, wide with confusion, shot up to meet his.

"I want to taste you." Needed to, desperately. Like he'd never needed anything before. Not a feeling he was used to, and not one he had the time—or the inclination—to examine with Noelle's mouth hovering mere inches from his dick, her hot breath washing over the head. "Straddle me."

"Now?"

"No time like the present."

After a moment's hesitation, she flipped around so her pussy was level with his face.

"Bon appétit." Jace pushed her panties aside with one finger and lifted his head to trail the tip of his tongue over her clit.

Christ, she was sweet. Wet and ready for him and so responsive, arching into him, demanding more even as she gave, taking him into her mouth and drawing him in until she engulfed him from root to tip.

He returned the favor, diving in and sucking her clit between his lips. She moaned, the hum traveling down his cock to his balls, making them pull up tight to his groin. She pressed her elbows into the bed on either side of him and released him long enough to beg.

"Please, Jace."

He wanted to take his time. Explore every inch of her body, find erogenous zones she didn't even know she had. But her needy noises—and his wrought-iron cock—were telling him a different story.

"Please," she moaned again, the word vibrating around his dick. She dragged a nail across his balls and they twitched in her palm. One finger inched dangerously close to his asshole.

Goddamn. He was going to blow any second if she kept that up.

"Are you ready, Duchess?" he lowered his head to ask. "I go, you go."

Her answer was another needy whimper. He licked her hard and fast, lapping up her release as she came, writhing and twisting, against his tongue. When she'd finished, he let himself go, pulling back to spill all over her breasts and belly.

"Ohmigod." She rolled off him, reversed position so her head was next to his and flopped onto her back, eyes closed, one arm flung across her forehead. "That was…"

"Epic?" He collapsed beside her. "Monumental? Earth–shattering? All of the above?"

"I'd say all of the above if I didn't think it would give you a swelled head."

"You liked my swelled head a minute ago."

"Wrong head." She turned to face him, a seductive smile playing on her lips. "Think a little farther north."

"No can do." He fingered his already recovering cock. "Little Jace is gearing up for round two."

"Little Jace might be ready, but I'm a mess." She glanced at her chest then down further to her stomach, both still wet and sticky from his orgasm, and rolled away from him.

"I've got a plan that will satisfy both of you." He reached across the bed, scooped her up and stood.

She squealed and clutched at his shoulders. God, he loved how she felt against him, lean and lithe but soft and warm. "Your arm…"

"…is fine," he finished for her as he crossed the room in two long strides. "You're not exactly a heavyweight. And we're not going far."

"Where are you taking me?"

"The bathroom, so you can get clean. Then we can get dirty again."

He kicked open the door, set her down and turned on the bathtub faucet. When the water was an appropriate temperature, he flipped the lever for the shower.

"One of us has too many clothes on." He plucked a condom from the medicine cabinet, set it on the edge of the tub and stepped under the spray.

Wordlessly, she reached behind her back and unfastened her bra. The lavender straps fell agonizingly slowly off her shoulders and down her arms.

"You might want to pick up the pace. I wouldn't want to run out of hot water before we're…"

"Finished?" she offered.

"Satisfied," he corrected.

She lowered her hands, and the scrap of lace fluttered to the floor. A second later, her panties followed.

His eyes flicked from the soft swell of her breasts to her taut stomach to the shadow at the junction of her legs. She was a feast, and he felt like he'd been starving for years.

"Damn near perfect." He held a hand out to her.

"Just near?" she joked, taking it and joining him in the shower. "I'm insulted."

He drew her under the spray and pulled the shower curtain shut. She closed her eyes, tipped her head back and let the water pour over her, darkening her ashen curls to almost brown.

"Feel good?"

"Mmm." She smoothed her hair back, the simple gesture thrusting her nipples skyward.

Whoa, big fella. Clean first, then dirty.

"Turn around, and I'll make it feel even better."

She complied eagerly. He grabbed the body wash off

the edge of the tub behind him, squirted some into his palm and worked it into a lather. Wrapping his arms around her, he soaped up her breasts and belly until she leaned limply against him, her head resting on his shoulder, his rigid cock jutting between her ass cheeks.

Steam engulfed them as he bent his head to kiss her. She met his lips, sighing into him, the sound audible even above the running water. His mouth moved over hers and he smoothed a hand down her front, rinsing her off.

"There," he said when he was finally able to pry his lips from hers. "All clean."

"What now?" she asked on a thin puff of air, like the kiss had stolen her breath away.

She tried to turn around to face him but his hands moved to her shoulders, stopping her. "Now I slide into you and pound that sweet pussy until you come."

"Yes, please." She braced herself against the wall, palms flat on the tile above her head, and spread her legs. "I need you inside me."

Her words tightened his balls and made his dick twitch. He loved how she told him exactly what she wanted, with her lips and her body. And as light and lean as she was, there was an underlying strength to her as she pushed back against him, demanding more.

He reached for the condom packet, tore it open and unrolled it over himself. The water beat down on them as he entered her in one swift stroke.

Damn, she felt good. Warm and wet and more than willing. And so fucking tight he almost lost it after a few thrusts like some inexperienced schoolboy. He gritted his teeth and tried to concentrate on something mundane, like batting averages and on-base percentages, but her desperate gasps and groans made it a losing battle.

He leaned in to her, covering her hands with one of

his and bringing the other around to massage her clit. She tilted her head back, letting him see how her eyes widened every time he pushed deep, burying himself to the balls.

"That's it, right there." Her muscles clenched around his cock, squeezing him, spurring him to thrust harder, faster.

He turned his head to plant a kiss on the sensitive spot where her collarbone met her neck as she came. With a shudder, he went with her, the arm around her waist banding her tightly to him.

"Holy shit," he said, resting his forehead against her damp hair.

"You can say that again."

He did, and she laughed. "The water's getting cold."

He reached behind him to turn it off then opened the shower curtain and grabbed two towels, wrapping one around her and scrubbing his hair with the other. "Problem solved. Now what do you say we get dry and try this the way God and nature intended?"

"And how's that?" she asked, fastening the towel between her breasts and following him out of the bathroom.

"Horizontal. In bed."

"I don't know." She bit her lip and pretended to study him seriously, but the playful glint in her eyes gave her away. "Sounds boring."

"You. Me. Naked. One thing's guaranteed, Duchess. It sure as hell won't be boring."

He took her hand and tugged her onto the bed. She settled in next to him and he pulled her close, front to front this time. She wiggled against him and gave a contented purr.

Definitely a home run in his book.

8

THREE QUICK RAPS at the door woke Noelle from the best
sleep she'd had in months. She blinked and rubbed her
eyes, unable to focus. What the heck time was it anyway?
And who was banging down her door?

Three more knocks, then a young, male voice. "Mr....
Jace?"

Jace?

She blinked again and rolled over, smack into a very
hard, very warm and very naked body.

Jace.

The events of the night before came rushing back. His
hands and mouth and that hard, warm, naked body all
over her, and vice versa. She'd climaxed not one, not two,
not even three but four times. More than she had with
Yannick in an entire month, never mind a single night.

One single, glorious night that was supposed to end
with her doing the walk of shame back to her room in the
wee hours, when the halls were virtually deserted. Except
that fourth orgasm had worn her out, and she'd overslept.

Way overslept.

"Jace," she hissed, nudging his shoulder and trying
to ignore how dead sexy he looked with his hair sleep-

rumpled and the sheet bunched around his waist, leaving her eyes free to roam over his beefy biceps, sculpted pecs and washboard abs. She balled her hands into fists to stop them from following suit. "Wake up."

"Ready for more?" He reached for her, his hand unerringly finding its target—her breast—and squeezing, his thumb grazing over her already hardening nipple. "What is this, round five? Six?"

"Try round nothing." Semi-reluctantly and extra-carefully thanks to her aching muscles—multiple orgasms would do that to a girl, even one who wasn't already injured—Noelle rolled away from Jace and off the bed, taking the sheet with her and wrapping herself in it. "Someone's at the door."

As if on cue, the knocking started again. "Is anyone there? It's me, Dylan."

"Dammit." Jace stood and pulled on his boxers. "I was supposed to meet him for breakfast."

"He can't see me here." Noelle scrambled to pick up her clothes—shirt sticking out from under the bed, yoga pants in a heap by the dresser, underwear thrown over the television—her sore muscles screaming at her with every move.

"Don't forget this." Jace dangled her bra from his fingertips.

"Not funny." She snatched it away.

"You can hide in the bathroom until I get rid of him."

"Make it quick." Clutching her clothes in one hand, she hoisted up the sheet with the other. "But be nice to that boy. He idolizes you."

"Yes, ma'am." He gave her a mock salute. "I'll tell him to meet me in the dining room in five minutes."

He lifted his arm and sniffed, wrinkling his nose. "Make that ten."

Another series of knocks, harder this time. "I can hear you in there. Are you okay?"

"Just answer the door before he breaks it down." She stumbled into the bathroom, closing the door behind her. Slumping against it, she blew out a relieved sigh.

"Hey," Jace whispered through the crack, making her jump and almost drop her clothes and the sheet. "You missed something."

She opened the door a hair and he shoved her leg brace through.

"Thanks." She slammed the door shut the second his arm was clear.

"Is everything all right in there?" Dylan called.

"Be with you in a sec," Jace answered. Noelle could hear him moving away. "Just getting dressed."

After a few thumps, presumably Jace hunting down something more than a pair of boxer shorts, she heard him answer the door. She tuned out the rest of his conversation with Dylan and concentrated on making herself presentable, starting with ditching the sheet for her tank top and yoga pants. She'd adjusted her brace and was slipping her pants on over it when Jace spoke through the crack in the bathroom door again.

"Okay, Duchess. You can come out now. The coast is clear."

She pulled her tank top down over her head. "That was fast."

"I work fast."

He could say that again. They'd only known each other a couple of weeks. Never even gone out on a date, unless you counted walking around the clinic and sharing macaroons, which she didn't. And yet she'd let him touch her in ways no man ever had. Not just let him. Begged him.

Heat crept up her cheeks at the memory. She caught a

glimpse of herself in the bathroom mirror and frowned. Not only was her face beet-red, her hair looked like a family of rats had moved in and thrown a party, and she hadn't brushed her teeth in almost twelve hours.

"Almost done in here." She found Jace's toothpaste on the counter top, squirted a dollop on her finger and ran it across her teeth. Her hair might be beyond hope, but her breath could still be saved. When she was done, she rinsed her mouth and splashed her face with cold water.

"All yours," she said as she opened the door and brushed past him.

"Thanks." He got halfway through before turning back to her. His chest still bare, he'd put on jeans but neglected to button them, and she could see a tantalizing slice of his happy trail over the waistband of his boxers. "We okay?"

"Sure." She shrugged, hoping the lie didn't show on her face. "Why wouldn't we be?"

"You know why."

"It's all good. We scratched an itch. Now we can move on." She spotted her ballet flats in the corner by the window and bent to pick them up, saying a silent prayer that Dylan hadn't made it far enough into the room to see them, too.

Jace chuckled behind her, no doubt getting an eyeful of her backside. "Honey, this is way more than an itch. I'm talking full-on poison ivy. Or maybe chicken pox. Whichever is worse. It's gonna take more than one little scratch."

She sat on the bed and slid her feet into her shoes. "I seem to recall four 'little scratches' over the course of the night. That wasn't enough?"

"Not for me. Can you honestly say it was for you?"

No, she honestly couldn't. But there were a whole host

of other reasons why continuing to scratch their so-called itch was a bad idea. For example…

"We can't keep doing this. What if someone found out?"

"What if they did?" He leaned against the doorframe and folded his massive arms across his naked chest, almost making her objections fly out the window. Almost. "Would that be so awful? We're two consenting adults. I've got nothing to hide."

"You may not, but I do. I've got a reputation to uphold."

"And I don't?"

"Are you kidding? You're the bad boy of baseball. Your reputation is safe and sound. Whereas mine…" She hesitated, debating how much to admit to him and deciding to keep it to a minimum. "My last breakup wasn't pretty. The press had a field day. I can't go through that again."

The headlines flashed across her brain like the news ticker in Times Square.

Behind The Scenes Drama Takes Center Stage At NYC Ballet.

Ballerinas, Choreographer Caught In NYCB Love Triangle.

Duped And Dumped! What Will Prima Ballerina Noelle Nelson's Very Public Split With Choreographer Yannick Grenier Mean For Her Career?

"And you won't." With a shrug of one shoulder, Jace brushed off her concern. "We'll keep things on the downlow."

Noelle stood and straightened her shirt. "Do you really think that's possible?"

"Why not? This place prides itself on its privacy. No one knows we're here but our friends and family."

"What about the staff? And the other patients?"

He stalked over to her, all sex appeal and smolder, and took her chin in his hand. "We'll be discreet. And if someone does happen to see something, they'll keep their mouth shut or risk getting thrown out on their ass."

"The clinic would do that?"

"In a New York minute." He brushed a thumb over her cheekbone, starting a ripple of lust that went all the way down to her toes. "So what do you say? You in?"

"I'll… I'll get back to you on that." She shook her head and stepped away, breaking his pseudo-hypnotic contact. "Now go. Get ready. Dylan won't wait forever."

"Neither will I, sweetness." He winked and headed for the bathroom, calling over his shoulder as he went. "Neither will I."

IT WAS MORE like thirty minutes than ten by the time Jace made it to the dining room. Just a fancy name for a cafeteria, really. Moving slower than a three-hundred-pound defensive lineman thanks to the marathon sex session—Sara was going to ream his ass out in PT—he grabbed a tray, loaded it up with scrambled eggs, bacon, toast and coffee and scanned the room for Dylan.

He found him at a table in the corner. Not hard, since the kid was waving like a madman to get his attention. He was patient, Jace would give him that. And eager.

"Hey, Dylan. Sorry I kept you waiting." Jace plunked down his tray and pulled a manila envelope out from under his arm. "But I brought you something to make up for it."

He tossed the envelope down on the table in front of the teenager.

Dylan held it steady with what remained of his left arm and undid the clasp with his right. "Thanks."

"Don't get too excited," Jace warned, taking a seat across the table. "It's not a signed baseball or anything."

Not that he hadn't thought of that. He'd already tasked Coop with bringing a shitload of Storm memorabilia when he came out in a couple of weeks at the All-Star break.

Dylan smiled and blew his bangs off his forehead. "I kind of figured from the package."

He struggled to open the flap, finally succeeding and pulling out a stack of papers.

"I printed some stuff off the internet," Jace explained. "It was the best I could do on short notice."

Dylan thumbed through the pile. "Jim Abbott. Pete Gray. Those are the guys you mentioned yesterday, aren't they?"

Jace nodded and chugged his coffee. "I ordered some books from Amazon, but they won't get here for a few days. I figured this would give you a head start."

"Head start? On what?"

"Getting back on the mound."

"I don't know if you've noticed, but I'm kind of missing an arm here." Dylan lifted his stump.

"So were Abbott and Gray. And they played in the majors."

"Seriously?"

"Abbott was a pitcher, like you. Even threw a no-hitter."

"No way."

"Yes way." Jace tapped the stack of papers. "Read all about it. Then we can talk."

"You bet." The kid stuck the papers back in the envelope, shoveled the last of his eggs into his mouth and washed them down with orange juice.

Jace tucked into his breakfast and listened to Dylan

talk baseball, rattling off statistics like Vin Scully. If Dylan didn't beat the odds and make it back on the field—which, okay, was a major long shot, despite what Abbott and Gray had accomplished—he'd make one hell of a sportscaster.

Dylan was midway through his recap of game seven of the 2001 World Series—he would have been what? One? Two?—when Jace felt the hairs at the back of his neck prickle. Even before he saw her out of the corner of his eye, he knew.

Noelle.

She hobbled her way down the food line, somehow managing to look graceful as she tried to balance her tray, still favoring her injured leg. She'd tamed her hair—barely—and put on a fresh set of clothes and a touch of makeup, but even across the room she had the unmistakable, well-pleased glow of a woman who'd been thoroughly ravished the night before.

By him.

Jace cleared his throat and dragged his eyes back to his plate. He'd promised to be discreet, and the last time he checked public leering wasn't part of the dictionary definition.

"She's pretty, huh? She your girlfriend?"

Shit. So much for discretion.

"Friend."

"I think she's into you," Dylan observed as she threaded through the tables to a seat on the other side of the room. "She was totally down with you in the hall yesterday."

"Down with me?"

"Yeah, she digs you. Trust me." Dylan swiveled back around to Jace. "You should ask her out."

If he only knew. "You think so?"

"Sure. What have you got to lose?"

Great. Just great. Now he was getting dating advice from a kid who'd barely started dating himself.

"Besides," Dylan continued, "there's not much else to do in this joint."

True that. Jace ran his fork through what was left of his eggs and played along. "And where, pray tell, should I take the lovely lady? We're in the middle of nowhere here."

It was twenty miles to the nearest town, if you called an intersection with a gas station, mini-mart and municipal building that served as the police station/post office/county courthouse a town, and Phoenix was a two-hour drive. Great for keeping the paparazzi and lookie loos away but hell on the social life.

Dylan half lifted a shoulder and peered out through too-long bangs. How the kid found the strike zone with that shit in his eyes was beyond Jace. "It doesn't have to be anything fancy. What's she into? Other than you, I mean. Girls dig it when you pay attention to stuff they like."

Damn. Kid had game. Maybe Jace could learn something from him after all.

He stared at Noelle across the cafeteria, as far from him as she could get and still be in the same room. Her parting words to him that morning were a challenge, one he was all too willing to accept. He wasn't the type to sit on his hands and wait for a woman—or anyone—to "get back to" him.

It was two outs, two strikes, bottom of the ninth. Time for him to hit one out of the park.

He turned to Dylan. "I've got an idea. But I'm going to need help."

"Sure thing." The teenager lit up like he'd struck out

the side in front of a capacity crowd at Fenway. "Whatever you need, I'm your man."

"Great." Jace downed the rest of his coffee, picked up his tray and stood. "Let's get started. First things first. We need to make an appointment with the hairdresser. She's usually here on Tuesdays and Thursdays."

"Oh, I get it. You want to look dope before you make your move." Dylan put the manila envelope on his tray, one-handed the whole thing and followed Jace across the room. The kid was adapting quickly, even without a prosthetic. Good sign.

"Not me, hotshot. You."

Dylan put his tray on the conveyor belt leading back to the kitchen and ran a hand through his shaggy blond locks, remembering at the last minute to snag the envelope back before the tray moved too far down the line. "I always look dope."

Ah, the blind confidence of youth.

Jace set his tray down behind Dylan's and watched them both disappear. "That may be true, but you can't play ball with your hair in your eyes."

Christ. He was barely thirty years old. When had he become his father?

Dylan gave him a blank stare. "I thought this was about you and the ballerina chick."

"It is. But that doesn't mean I can't give you a little friendly advice." Jace clapped the boy's shoulder and led him into the hallway. "So what do you say?"

"Okay," Dylan said after a moment's thought, drawing the word out like it was four syllables instead of two. "Just don't let her make me look like a total gomer."

"Sure, kid." Whatever that was. Damn, he was turning into his father. "Sure."

9

"MISS NELSON! MISS NELSON!"

Noelle turned to find Dylan sprinting down the hall toward her.

"Slow down, buddy," she teased. "Where's the fire?"

He pulled up short next to her. "Sorry, I just wanted to make sure I caught up with you so I could give you these."

He held out a delicate bouquet of flowers in varying shades of pink, purple, orange and yellow.

Noelle took an uncomfortable step back, shoving her hands in her pockets. It wasn't the first time she'd had to let down a starstruck fan with a crush, but it never got any easier. Especially when said fan was an impressionable teen. "Dylan, you shouldn't have…"

"I didn't." He thrust the flowers at her. "Read the card."

She took the bouquet, fished out an envelope from among the blooms and slit it open with her finger, reading silently.

Follow the kid. Don't ask questions.

"Who sent this?" Like she didn't know. Only one smug, self-important, sinfully sexy shortstop was bold enough to order her around like a drill sergeant.

"He told me not to say." Dylan looked down at his Air Jordans. "And that you should come with me, no questions asked. That's what the note says, right?"

"I'm not one to blindly follow orders." Even if they were from the man who'd given her her only non-self-induced orgasm in the past six months.

"He also told me you might be less than agreeable. And if you were, I should give you this."

Dylan pulled out another envelope and handed it to her. Noelle ripped it open impatiently and mouthed the single word on the card.

Please.

Damn him. All her righteous indignation seeped out of her, curiosity rushing in to take its place. What did Jace have up his sleeve now?

"All right, lead on." She gestured for Dylan to go ahead, cringing a little inside when he took her past the pool. "Any idea what Ja—uh, the man who sent you has planned? I was hoping to squeeze in a late-night swim."

She'd been doing that a lot lately. Sara said it was a great low-impact, non-weight-bearing workout. And Noelle could swim longer, and with less pain, than with any other activity.

Dylan gave her an oh-no-you-didn't finger wave. "No questions, remember?"

With a resigned sigh, she followed him to the lobby. But instead of crossing through to the other side of the clinic, like she expected, he headed for the main doors. Outside, she could see a sleek, cherry-red, classic sports car parked at the curb and an equally slick shortstop lounging against it. His gaze met hers, and his face split wide in a shit-eating grin.

She came to a quick halt, careful even in her rapidly escalating pissed-off state not to jar her knee. He'd gotten

the same spiel on admission as every other patient. Twice, since he was a repeat customer. No going off the grounds without prior permission. Mr. Hotshot Major Leaguer might think he was above the rules, but she didn't.

"Hold the damn phone," she said, talking to Dylan but her eyes never leaving Jace, boring holes through his skull through the closed door. "You never said anything about leaving the clinic."

Dylan looked over his shoulder and smiled. "I never said anything, period. But don't worry, he'll fill you in."

The teen took a step toward the automatic doors and they slid open, belting her with a blast of hot, July air. Whoever said it was the humidity, not the heat, that made you miserable had never spent a summer in Arizona. Hot was hot, humid or not.

"I am not going out there." She planted her feet wide.

"She says she's not going out there," Dylan called through the door.

"Thanks, man," Jace called back, not bothering to move from his relaxed stance against the car. "I've got it from here."

"That's what you think," Noelle muttered as Dylan gave Jace a thumbs-up and took off.

"I mean it," she said, louder this time so Jace could hear her. "I'm not going out there."

The doors started to close, but Jace sprang forward and stuck out his hand, stopping them. "Give me one good reason."

"I'll give you two." She held up a finger. "One, it's hot as hell. And two—" she added another digit "—I don't have medical authorization to leave."

"Easy." Jace crossed back to the curb in two strides and thumped the roof of the car. "I've got the air condi-

tioning in this baby cranked as high as it'll go and a note from Sara springing you for a few hours."

"A few hours?" Almost unconsciously, Noelle stepped outside, feeling the doors whoosh shut behind her. "Where do you think you're taking me?"

"Only one way to find out." He sauntered around to the passenger side and opened the door. "Hop in."

She crossed her arms and stood firm. "Not until I see the note."

"Don't trust me?" he asked, one brow raised.

"Bingo."

"I'm wounded." He staggered back and put a hand to his heart like he'd been shot, but when he was done with the theatrics he produced a crumpled piece of paper from his pants pocket and handed it to her.

She smoothed it out and studied it carefully before looking up at Jace, who was half sitting, half leaning on the hood of the car. The man was like a Bengal tiger, coiled and ready to spring. Long legs crossed at the ankles, arms folded over his massive chest and those biceps—*gah*. She had to look away before words would form. "It looks legit. You're sure Sara's okay with this?"

"Her exact words were, 'Get her out of here. That girl needs a change of scenery, stat.'"

"Sounds like Sara," Noelle conceded with a wry chuckle.

"So what's the verdict? You coming?"

As much as Noelle hated to admit it, Sara made sense. She'd been starting to go a little stir-crazy cooped up at the clinic. Last week, she'd even resorted to pulling out a needlepoint kit her well-intentioned but delusional mother had sent her. A ladybug pillow. Seriously, who under the age of sixty did that stuff any more?

She did, apparently, if she got desperate enough.

She didn't want to be that desperate. And how much damage could one night out do, even if it was with Jace? Heck, she'd already slept with him. Things couldn't get any more complicated.

Could they?

"Okay," she said, throwing caution out the window and into the arid desert. "But this doesn't mean we're an item."

"An item?" He snickered. "What is this, high school?"

"Fine. We're not a couple, then."

"Understood." He rushed to beat her to the still open passenger door. "Now can we blow this popcorn stand?"

She looked down at her outfit. Athletic shirt, yoga pants, sneakers. Standard attire at Spaulding. But probably not for whatever Jace had in store for her. "I have to change."

"Don't go changing to try and please me."

"It's not for you, Billy Joel. It's for me."

"Whatever butters your bagel." *Yeah, right.* Like she ate bagels. Way too many carbs. "But make it snappy. We've got a schedule to keep."

"Want to give me a hint as to the dress code?"

His eyes raked her up and down. "Like I said, you look fine to me."

Typical guy.

"Some help you are." She mentally cataloged the meager inventory of her closet. She hadn't brought along much more than workout clothes, but she'd thrown in a cute little two-piece skater dress and a pair of jeweled Gucci thong sandals at the last minute that should work for whatever he had planned. After all, it wasn't like they were going to be horseback riding or skydiving with their respective injuries. "Be back in ten."

"You won't regret it, I promise," he called after her as she went in.

That remained to be seen. With an uber alpha male like Jace Monroe, anything was possible. She held in a breath, the thought both exciting and terrifying her.

And she didn't know which of those warring emotions she wanted to win out.

"HERE WE ARE."

Jace pulled the 1965 Mustang GT to a stop, almost disappointed the drive was over.

What a sweet ride. And he didn't just mean the expensive rental.

Two hours was a long time to be trapped in a car with someone, especially a car with quarters as tight as the Mustang. And as intimate as he and Noelle had been, they hadn't exactly done a lot of talking.

Until now.

Her large, loud family. His father. Their respective careers. Even normally off-limits topics like politics (Republican for him, Democrat for her) and religion (she was a lapsed Catholic, he an agnostic). Despite their differences, not once had the conversation turned ugly or lagged. And not once could he remember a conversation with a woman—just conversation—being so…stimulating.

"Phoenix Fright Fest." Noelle read the marquis on the historic downtown theater they were parked in front of. "Is that where we're going?"

He studied her for some reaction. He'd gone out on a big-ass limb bringing her all this way on the basis of nothing more than a random comment in a years-old interview with some podunk newspaper.

Her head swiveled slowly away from the window, her

jaw slack and her eyes uncertain as they turned on him. "You drove over a hundred miles to take me to a slasher flick?"

The big-ass limb cracked underneath him.

"Not just any slasher flick," he scrambled to explain. "It's…"

"Are you kidding?" She cut him off, her voice rising to a decibel level only dogs could hear. "I love horror movies. They're my guilty pleasure. No matter what hotel you're in, in what city, you can always find one with the click of a remote from the comfort of your bed."

"Kind of like porn." He slipped a finger under the strap of her dress.

"Like you said, whatever butters your bagel." She slapped his hand away. "How did you know?"

"About the porn?"

"No, smartass." She unbuckled her seat belt. "About my secret, borderline unhealthy obsession with horror movies. It's not something I usually share. My agent says it doesn't fit the public image of a ballerina. I'm supposed to be the cultural icon of idealized femininity, or some crap like that. I think he read it somewhere."

She was babbling, almost bouncing out of her seat, and it was unexpected, uncharacteristic and utterly adorable. *Score.*

"The magic of the World Wide Web. You mentioned it in an interview you gave to a small-town newspaper a few years back." Turned out Dylan wasn't just a crack pitcher, he was a computer whiz, too. A few creative searches and he'd managed to not only dredge up the long-ago article but find the website for Fright Fest as well.

"Must have been before Garrett put the gag order on me." Noelle fumbled under her legs for her purse. "So are we going to sit here all night or go in?"

"Go in." He exited the Mustang, went around to the passenger side and opened her door. "You ain't seen nothin' yet."

"There's more?"

"Patience, Duchess. Patience."

He ushered her through the lobby to the ticket taker, a spiky-haired twenty-something who stared at Jace open-mouthed.

"Ohmigod, you're..."

"Shhh." Jace put a finger to his lips and handed their tickets over. "Give us a break, okay, man? We just want to enjoy the movie on the down-low."

He held his breath as Spiky Hair studied them. He was used to being recognized in California, where the Storm played, but farther from his home base he was usually able to fly under the radar. Leave it to lady luck to put a baseball buff at the door.

"You bet," the usher said after a beat. "Let's get you inside. No one will recognize you in the dark."

He looked at the tickets. "Sweet. VIP passes. Right this way, Mr. Monroe."

The usher led them to the front of the theater, where the first few rows were corded off. He unhitched the rope and let them pass, showing them to two seats in the second row on the aisle.

"Here you go." He handed their passes back, along with two programs. "Enjoy the show. The VIP reception and talkback with Mr. Carpenter will be immediately afterward, upstairs in the green room. It's all in your handouts."

"Mr. Carpenter?" Noelle asked as the usher made his way back up the aisle. "Does he mean... ?"

"Yep. John Carpenter, the greatest living horror director. At least according to Dylan."

"Dylan was in on this, too?"

She tensed a little, her lips pressing into a thin line, and he knew immediately what she was thinking. Funny how quickly he'd learned to read her. "Don't worry. As far as Dylan and Sara know, we're just two friends cutting loose and blowing off some steam."

She relaxed and put a hand on his thigh, dangerously close to his groin. Now he was the one getting stiff. "We're really going to meet John Carpenter?"

"Surprise." Jace covered her hand with his and leaned in to whisper in her ear as the lights went down. "Told you you hadn't seen anything yet."

"Thank you," she whispered back, her voice barely audible over the creepy opening theme.

It had been ages since he'd been to a horror flick. They weren't his thing. Give him a sci-fi or superhero movie any day. But within minutes, he remembered why they'd been so popular when he was in high school.

"Don't go in the garage." Noelle snuggled close and gripped his hand as the girl on the screen ignored her advice and opened the car door. "He's in the backseat."

True to her word, the white-masked killer popped up and Noelle jumped, clutching Jace harder and burying her face in his shoulder. The fresh, flowery scent of her perfume or shampoo surrounded him.

"You have seen this movie before, haven't you?" he asked with a chuckle.

"Of course." He could almost hear her smile in the dark. "But the good ones always make you jump, no matter how many times you've seen them."

They watched the rest of the movie in relative silence save for her gasps and screams every time another victim met their grisly end. With each killing, she cuddled closer. The body count was high so by the end of the

flick she would have been in his lap if there wasn't an arm rest between them.

And his dick was as hard as a steel rod, creating an uncomfortable bulge in his jeans. He shifted away from her and adjusted himself before the lights went up.

"Now comes the real treat. Ready to meet the man of the hour?" He stood and held out a hand to her.

She took it, standing and brushing her lips against his cheek in a kiss so gentle he almost missed it. "I'm more than ready to meet Mr. Carpenter. But the man of the hour is the guy who went through all the trouble to set this up. And that's the real treat."

10

NOELLE FLOATED OUT of the theater on a cloud of contentment. No, contentment wasn't a strong enough word. Euphoria was more like it. All because of the conundrum wrapped in an enigma that was Jace Monroe. Superstar shortstop. Legendary ladies' man. The man on the back of baseball cards and the front of cereal boxes who'd taken the time to discover her guilty pleasure and give her a night she'd never forget.

She didn't want to admit it, but he'd gotten to her. How could he not? No other man had ever gone to such lengths to please her, inside the bedroom or out. Yet Jace had figured out how to do both in the span of only a few weeks.

"After you." He swung open the passenger door of the sports car and helped her in.

"Thanks again," she said when he'd settled into the driver's seat. "For everything. I can't believe you did all this for me."

He turned the key and the engine started with a roar. "Would it tarnish your newly shiny image of me if I told you my motives weren't entirely pure?"

"Only a little." She fastened her seat belt and stretched out her bum leg. "Any man who'd go to the lengths you

did just to get into my pants deserves a certain amount of consideration."

"Hey, I never said it was just to get into your pants."

"So you admit you want to get into my pants."

"Don't you mean get into your pants again?"

"Semantics."

Jace smoothly maneuvered the sports car into traffic. "So, was meeting the prince of darkness all you thought it would be?"

"And more." The director had been charming, funny and generous to a fault with his time, answering questions and signing autographs long after he was supposed to leave. She smoothed a hand over the program in her lap, tracing the letters in his signature then tucking it safely in her purse. "I'm still a bit starstruck."

"Now you know how your fans feel."

"And yours." She leaned her head back and closed her eyes, fighting a yawn.

"Tired, Duchess?"

"More than I realized until this second."

"Then sit back, relax and get some sleep. I'll wake you when we're home."

"Home?" She cracked one eye open and turned her head to look at him.

"You know what I mean." He pulled up at a stop light. "Mind if I put the top down?"

"Sure, why not? It's a nice night."

"Not worried about messing up your hair?" He reached above him with both hands, released a latch, then hit a button on the dash, retracting the roof.

"Nah." She shut her eye and let out a contented sigh. "I rock the windswept look."

"I'll bet you do."

She heard the engine rev and felt the wind pick up.

The steady hum of the motor relaxed her and within a few minutes she could feel herself drifting off to sleep.

It could have been ten minutes or two hours when she woke up with her head on Jace's shoulder, one hand pressed against the rough denim of his jeans.

And that wasn't the only thing it was pressing against.

A slow, answering ache stirred inside her, starting in her belly and working its way up to her chest. Almost involuntarily, her hand curled around his thigh.

"Don't. Move." He jerked the steering wheel and the car made a sharp right.

"Hey!" Her grip tightened on his thigh, making his erection twitch under her fingertips.

"I'm not kidding, Duchess. One more inch and I'm gonna bust a nut, run us off the road or both." Another turn and gravel crunched under the tires.

"What are you doing?"

"Making sure I don't kill us." He slowed the car to a stop, turned off the ignition and slid the bench seat back.

She sat up and peered out the windshield. He'd parked at the edge of a field, nothing but darkness and the silhouettes of the acacia trees in the distance. "Where are we?"

"Somewhere no one will see me do this."

He slid across the seat, pinning her against the door with his hot, hard body and claiming her mouth in a scorching, demanding kiss. He framed her face in his big, work-roughened palms and pressed a thumb just below her jawline, where she was sure he could feel her pulse racing like a member of the corps de ballet dancing her first solo.

She kissed him back, openmouthed, her tongue sliding against his. She focused her attention on the magic he was making with his lips and fingers, trying to blur

out the niggling fear they'd be discovered by some un-suspecting dog walker or, even worse, a police officer.

"You're thinking too much," Jace scolded, breaking off the kiss. He worked one hand under the top part of her dress and cupped her breast through the lace of her bra. His thumb found her nipple and circled it, teasing.

A zing of pleasure rippled through her and she dropped her head back against the seat. "I do that a lot."

"Stop." His forefinger joined his thumb and squeezed. "The only thing I want you doing right now is feeling."

"Feeling what?" She closed her eyes and let the sensations emanating from his fingers wash over her.

"This." He tugged at her nipple, the brief but sharp pinch of pain surprisingly stimulating.

"And this." He nipped her earlobe, another twinge of sexual torture that sent shivers dancing down her spine.

"And this." His tongue soothed the ache his teeth had caused.

She threaded her fingers into his hair, holding him to her as his mouth caressed a path from the sensitive spot behind her ear to her collarbone. She was feeling, all right, like she'd never freaking felt before. It was all so…naughty. The pleasure/pain. The open air. The perverse thrill of knowing they could be interrupted at any moment.

Hot damn. Sex *en plein air* was fun.

"Top off," he growled.

She raised her arms and he yanked the flimsy garment over her head.

"Don't want to lose this." He tossed it into the back-seat and returned to worshiping her breasts, now clad in only her lacy bra, her nipples practically poking holes through the fabric.

She arched her back, a low hiss escaping from between her teeth. "You've obviously done this before."

"I'm no saint," he admitted, his fingers finding and fondling the already hardened nubs. "But I can honestly say I've never been so turned on I had to pull the car off the road."

"Nice to know." Her toes curled and her body tensed as his lips joined his fingers.

That was the last of the talking for a while as they divested themselves of as much of their clothes as they dared. His shirt went the way of her top, as did her panties. He unbuttoned his jeans and pushed them down past his hips.

"Condom," he grunted. "In my wallet. Right rear pocket."

He lifted his ass and she reached underneath him to pull it out, taking a second to cop a quick feel. He really did have a magnificent butt, round, firm and eminently squeezable.

"Quit stalling and hand it over." He snatched the condom from her, ripped it open and sheathed himself, pulling her into his lap when he was done.

She straddled him, hovering over his erection, pointed straight at the cloudless night sky. "You don't waste time, do you?"

"There's only one way to have public sex, sweetness." He gripped her hips and thrust upward, into her. "Quick and dirty. But don't worry. We'll try nice and slow later."

"LATER?" NOELLE PANTED, poised above him, her body flushed with arousal.

Jace began to move, long, fast strokes that had her moving, too, grinding against him, working her body, taking what she needed. She felt so fucking good, hot and

wet and tight, he wasn't going to last worth a damn. He was a greedy bastard, thinking of their next time before they'd even finished. But having her again, and taking his time to touch, taste and explore wasn't just a matter of want or even desire. It was a necessity. Like breathing.

"My room," he managed to grunt between thrusts. "You're staying with me tonight."

"Bossy, aren't we?" she asked, her gorgeous blond hair—and her equally beautiful breasts—bouncing wildly each time he pounded into her.

He slowed to catch his breath so he could answer. "You have a better idea?"

"Yes." She rested her forehead on his, almost speaking into his mouth. "My room. No rabid teenage baseball fans to interrupt us."

"Deal." He began moving again, the hands on her hips pulling down as he thrust hard. "Now shut up and come for me."

Wordlessly, they found a rhythm that brought them both to the edge. Noelle toppled over first, collapsing against him, burying her face in his shoulder and moaning her release into his neck. Her body still pulsing with the aftershocks of her orgasm, she kissed first his shoulder blade, then the hollow at the base of his throat, then his chest, her tongue daring to steal out and tease one nipple.

The tongue thing was the final straw for Jace. He let out an animal groan as he came, the muscles in his chest and abs tensing as jolt after jolt of pure pleasure shot through him.

When he was spent, he slumped in the seat, taking her with him. One hand trailed absently down her back, tracing the curve of her spine. "Is it my imagination, or does it get better every time?"

"It's not your imagination." She twirled a finger in his hair.

"How about we test that theory?"

"What do you suggest?"

He glanced into the backseat. Her top was on the floor behind him, his on the seat above it and her panties had somehow wound up hanging from the door handle. "For starters, putting our clothes back on."

"Sort of counterintuitive, isn't it?"

"Only so we can get back to Spaulding without being arrested before we hit your room and take them off again."

"Well, why didn't you say so in the first place?" She rolled off him and leaned over the seat to reach into the back of the car. "Get moving, superstar. We're wasting the wee hours."

He sat motionless. He could barely remember his damn name at the moment, with the bottom of her dress creeping up and that ass he loved, still sans panties, inches from his mouth, begging for him to take a bite. Or maybe that was him begging.

She sank back down onto the front seat, delivering him from temptation, and held his T-shirt out to him. "I meant what I said before. We have to keep this quiet. I won't become fodder for the tabloids again."

He took the shirt and shrugged it over his head. "Works for me. Nothing kills a comeback faster than bad press."

"You're telling me." She struggled to put her top on then squirmed into her panties. He moved in to seal the deal with a fast, hard kiss then started the car.

It was only about half an hour later when they pulled up in front of Spaulding.

"Seriously?" She ran a hand through her windblown

hair. "We were thirty minutes away and you couldn't wait until we got here to have sex?"

"What can I say? You inspire me." He hopped out of the convertible Steve McQueen style, vaulting over the closed door, and went around to the passenger side to help her out. He might not have had a mother growing up, but his father had taught him how to treat a lady. And Noelle Nelson was a lady from the blondest of the blond hairs on the top of her head to the tips of her battle-scarred dancer's toes.

"What about the car? It's a loaner, right? Don't you have to return it?"

"Someone's coming to pick it up in the morning." He opened the passenger door and held out a hand.

She took it, letting him pull her from the car. "Door-to-door service?"

"One of the perks of fame."

"Ah, yes," she said as they walked toward the main entrance, still holding hands like an old married couple. "But are they worth the price?"

Good question. His mother would say yes. So would most of the women he'd been with since joining the Storm. Ballpark bunnies, the guys called them, in it for the lavish lifestyle that came with dating—or, even better, marrying—a major leaguer.

But Noelle was cut from a different cloth. She had fame in her own right, and she'd seen the seedy side of living in the public eye. She wouldn't drop him like a bad habit when his career was over.

Wait. Whoa. Where did that thought come from? Number one, nobody was dropping anybody because, in Noelle's words, they were not "an item." And number two, his career was far from over.

As they neared the entrance, Noelle's steps slowed and

she released his hand, leaving him strangely empty and uncertain, two emotions he wasn't used to dealing with when it came to women.

Snap out of it, Monroe.

"What's wrong?" He measured his pace to match hers.

"We can't walk in together." She stopped, and he drew up alongside her.

"Why not?"

Her eyes darted to the glass door leading to the lobby, a silhouette clearly visible behind the reception desk. She pulled him into the shadow of the building where no one could see them. "It's late. People will talk."

"What people?"

"The night shift. Insomniacs."

He rubbed the back of his neck. It had been a long night, and he was hoping it would be a lot longer. But in her bed, not standing outside hiding like a couple of guilty teenagers. "So what do you suggest?"

"I'll go first. You follow in, say, five minutes." She moved out of the shadows toward the entrance but stopped after a few steps and turned back to him. "Make it ten. It's like Grand Central Station at reception all of a sudden."

"What am I supposed to do out here for ten minutes?"

Her gaze drifted downward, lingering for a second on his zipper before shooting back to his face. "I'm sure you'll think of something."

"Don't even go there. The next time I whip my pants down, it's going to be in the privacy of your room."

"Go where?" Her voice had the innocence of an angel, but her eyes flashed with devilish amusement. "I was talking about counting the stars. Or catching fireflies."

"Sure you were." He reached out and grabbed her wrist, tugging her back into the murky darkness. Then

he kissed her, quick and demanding, with just a hint of tongue to keep her guessing. "Ten minutes, Duchess. Be waiting. And be naked."

11

"I WIN." JACE PUMPED a fist in the air as he reached what Noelle had come to think of as "their" bench, which he had designated as the finish line. "Again."

"It was hardly a fair fight." She lagged behind him, panting. "You've got two good legs. I've only got one."

He ignored the comparison, running in circles around her as she finally crossed the imaginary wire. "How about another lap? I'll take it easy on you this time. Maybe even let you win."

"Give me a few minutes to recover." She sank onto the bench and stretched out her bum leg, rubbing the knee through her brace. Ever since Sara had told her it was okay to start running again, she and Jace had been doing laps around the building in the early evenings, when the sun had started to dip below the horizon and the heat became somewhat bearable. But today he'd decided to kick things up a notch and turn their casual jog into a no-holds-barred competition.

It was a challenge she couldn't back down from, even though she was certain to lose.

"Hydrate," he ordered, sitting next to her and detaching his water bottle from the strap around his waist.

She followed suit, taking a long gulp from her own bottle, and studied the tattoos running from his shoulder to his wrist. He hadn't put his brace on this morning—with or without Sara's blessing Noelle wasn't sure and didn't want to know—and they were clearly visible in his tank top. Plus she'd had plenty of time to study them at night, too. His tats didn't stop with his arm. They covered his right pec and even extended down his back to the bottom of his shoulder blade.

"Take a picture." With a wink, he clipped his water bottle back onto his belt. "It lasts longer."

He lifted the hem of his shirt to wipe his forehead, giving her a glimpse of the intricate pattern on his chest. Predictably, her heart rate, which was just starting to slow from the race, kicked into high gear.

"Can I ask you a question?"

He lowered his shirt and smiled. "You just did."

"Another one."

"Shoot." He held his hands out, palms up. "I'm an open book."

"Why all the tattoos?"

He tilted his head and gave her a self-satisfied smirk. "Too wrong-side-of-the-tracks for you?"

"I've got nothing against tattoos. My sister-in-law is covered with them. I just wondered if yours had any special significance."

"They're a mix of tribal patterns, mostly Aztec and Samoan, some Mayan. I got the first one the last time I tore this baby, and it sort of mushroomed from there."

"Do you think you'll get any more?"

"Maybe. If I feel the need." He stretched, stood and held out a hand to her. "Come on. One more time around before you get too comfortable."

She leaned back, crossing her arms. "What if I said I'd changed my mind?"

"Then I'd say you don't get your reward."

"Reward?" She perked up. Knowing Jace, it probably involved chocolate body paint, whipped cream and fur-lined handcuffs, things she wouldn't have found appetizing in the bedroom a few weeks ago but that held infinite possibilities now. Sex with him was like nothing she'd known before, sometimes intense, sometimes playful. She never knew what to expect, except that they'd both wind up sweaty, sated and smiling. "Like what?"

"You'll have to do one more lap to find out."

"Fine." She tightened her ponytail and rose, stubbornly refusing to take his hand. "Slave driver."

They set off again at an only slightly slower clip than before. They had barely rounded the front of the building when a huge pickup truck pulling a shiny, silver Airstream trailer rumbled into view up the drive, "La Cucaracha" sounding from its horn.

She slowed to a stop, hands on her hips. "Please tell me that's not my reward."

The pickup pulled up to the curb and a light brown head poked out of the driver's window.

"More like my punishment," Jace muttered.

"Nice work, man." The cab door swung open and the driver jumped down. A little shorter and a lot leaner than Jace, but no less attractive, he strode over to them with the confidence of a man completely comfortable in his own skin. "Should have known you'd wind up with the hottest chick in the place."

"Friend of yours?" Noelle asked.

Jace nodded. "Unfortunately."

"Cooper Morgan, Sacramento Storm second base-

man." He flung an arm around Jace. "I'm the one who makes this guy look good on the field."

"No, that'd be me." A second, darker-haired man came around from the passenger side of the pickup. As he got closer, Noelle could see an angry scar on one cheek. Rather than detracting from his rugged good looks, it added a dangerous edge to his appeal. "Reid Montgomery. First base."

Jace frowned. "Not that I'm not thrilled to see you, but shouldn't you be in Atlanta getting ready for the All-Star game?"

Reid gave a half-hearted shrug. "I'm on the fifteen-day DL."

"DL?" Noelle wrinkled her nose. It was like they were speaking a foreign language.

"Disabled list," Cooper explained. "Our boy fouled a ball off his right leg and bruised the bone."

She grimaced. "I feel your pain." *Literally.*

"Tough break," Jace agreed. "How'd you manage to keep it out of the press?"

"It happened in our last game in DC. They just put me on the list last night. My guess is it'll hit any time now."

Reid pulled his cell phone from his back pocket, swiped the screen and started tapping away. Noelle assumed he was checking the net to see if news of his injury had leaked out. It was a feeling she remembered well, that looming sense of dread, waiting for the media vultures to swoop in.

Ballerina Injured In On-Stage Accident At Lincoln Center.

Injured Noelle Nelson Withdraws From NYCB's Don Quixote.

Torn ACL Sidelines NYCB Principal Noelle Nelson For Rest of Season, Return In Doubt.

Jace, apparently sensing the need for a change of topic, gestured toward the Airstream. "Nice wheels. Which one of you is taking up the RV lifestyle?"

"Neither," the shorter one—Cooper—answered. "It's Bucky's."

"Our manager," Jace cut in, acting as interpreter for her again.

"Bought it this year so his wife could follow him from stadium to stadium," Cooper continued. "It was either that, retire or divorce, according to him. They flew to Punta Cana for a couple of days of sun and surf. He asked us—well, me, before this joker decided to tag along—to drive it back to Sacramento for him. We've got a seven-game home stand coming off the break."

"Sweet." Jace whistled. "But you can't park it there."

"Who said anything about parking?" Cooper elbowed Jace in the ribs. "We're here to kidnap you."

"Kidnap?"

"How's two days of fishing at Lake Mead sound?"

Jace's eyes darted to Noelle.

"Your lady can come along if she wants," Reid said, stowing his phone in his pocket.

Her stomach did a little flip-flop. Jace's "lady." Was that what she was? What she wanted to be?

She mentally smacked herself upside the head. No good could come thinking along those lines. What was it Holly had said? Don't worry about Mr. Right, focus on Mr. Right Now. "We're just friends."

Cooper and Reid exchanged a skeptical glance, which Jace either missed or chose to ignore.

"I'm sure Noelle has better things to do than sit around watching us fish and fart." He ran a hand lightly down her arm, even that small gesture sending her mind skipping back down Mr. Right Lane.

Stupid mind.

"Sounds delightful, but I wouldn't dream of crashing your boys-only outing."

"It's almost dinnertime. Why don't we go into town for some grub?" Jace suggested. "There's a roadhouse on Route 20 that has decent food and a pretty good selection of beers on tap. We can head to the lake first thing in the morning."

"Count me in." Reid rubbed his hands together. "I'm starving."

"Sounds good to me," Cooper agreed. "But I thought you said we couldn't park the trailer here."

"Drive it around back. There's a lot you can leave it in."

"Aren't you forgetting something?" Noelle gave Jace a pointed look. "Sara."

"Who's Sara?" Reid asked with a leer. "You got another girl stashed someplace around here?"

"Our PT." Jace's lip curled in a twisted grimace. "She's a real taskmaster."

"Only because you never follow directions." The corners of Noelle's mouth lifted, too, but in amusement. "She's a peach to me."

"I sprung you for a few hours, didn't I? I can handle Sara." With a hand at the small of her back that caused a ripple effect of arousal, Jace steered Noelle toward the clinic, not giving her a chance to voice any more objections. "We'll meet you out back. Just give us a few minutes to shower and change."

"Together?" Reid's voice dripped with sexual sarcasm.

Noelle's stomach did a barrel roll, but Jace lobbed off the insinuation, tossing it over his shoulder like it was a soft ball. "You heard the lady. We're just friends. If we

were more than that, you'd be waiting a hell of a lot longer than a few minutes."

Just friends. Why did her words feel like a knife to her heart when Jace said them? It was her idea to keep what they were doing on the down-low. He was trying to respect her wishes, not shove her to the side like Yannick, who'd never wanted her to meet his family or any of his friends outside the ballet company.

Another red flag she'd ignored.

"Then it's a damn good thing you're not more than that," Reid called after them. "I don't think I'd last that long. I'm dying of hunger here. Seriously. Dying."

She thought she heard Jace mutter "drama queen" as the clinic doors whooshed open and they passed through.

THE PARKING LOT of Two Dollar Bill's was jam-packed when they pulled in about an hour later. Or, if you went by the neon sign on the roof, which was missing a couple of letters, Two Doll Bill's.

"Nice place." Reid's eyes flicked from the sputtering sign to the peeling paint to the muddy pickups parked in messy rows, gun racks proudly displayed in the rear windows. "If you like living dangerously."

"Hey, you're the one who's starving," Jace reminded his friend from the backseat. "But if you insist, we could drive another twenty miles to the next place. Which is pretty much the same as this one, except with more camouflage, backward baseball caps and chewing tobacco."

"What he meant to say is we can't wait to dine in this charming establishment." Cooper turned off the engine and pocketed the keys. "Isn't that right, Professor?"

"Professor?" Noelle asked.

Jace reached over the front seat and slugged Reid

on the shoulder. "Genius here graduated from Stanford summa cum laude. With a degree in chemical engineering."

"Gotta keep my options open. Can't play ball forever."

Cooper jerked his head toward the backseat and clocked Reid in the same spot Jace had only seconds before, ten times harder if the pained expression on Reid's face was anything to go by. "Guess they didn't teach tact at that fancy-schmancy school of yours."

"Sorry, man." Reid rubbed his arm and shot Jace an apologetic glance. "I didn't mean you were…"

Jace cut him off. "No worries."

Liar. Truth was, Jace was worried as hell. His therapy was going slower than he'd expected. Way slower. His last stint in rehab had been a walk around the bases compared to this. Arm strength, range of motion—nothing was where it needed to be if he was going to be back in uniform on opening day next season.

"Come on." He opened his door, jumped down and extended a hand to Noelle. "Enough of this depressing shit. Who wants to get the party started?"

The inside of Two Dollar Bill's wasn't much better than the outside. A huge oak bar with a copper top dominated one side of the room. Red vinyl booths, an ancient juke box and a postage-stamp-sized dance floor occupied the other. The whole place reeked of stale beer and cigarette smoke. But despite the questionable atmosphere—or maybe because of it—the place was wall-to-wall people.

"What, no mechanical bull?" quipped Cooper.

Reid eyed Jace with a raised brow. "Sure you don't want to reconsider?"

"Twenty more miles, bro," Jace reminded him.

As if on cue, Reid's stomach growled.

"What a bunch of babies." Noelle pushed past them, headed for the hostess station. "I'll put us in for a table."

"Damn." Cooper let out a low whistle. "I like her."

"Me, too," Reid agreed. "You've finally met your match, Monroe."

"I haven't met my anything." Jace stuffed his hands in the pockets of his jeans. "Repeat after me: Just. Friends."

"Repeat after me," Reid echoed. "Bull. Shit."

"Now, boys." Cooper, always the peacemaker, stepped between them. "Play nice."

"It's a half hour wait," Noelle said as she returned, a pager in one hand. "Let's get a drink at the bar. They'll buzz us when our table's ready. "

She shoved the pager in the pocket of her dress and left without waiting for an answer.

"I take it back," Cooper said, his eyes following Noelle's gently swaying ass with a gleam of appreciation that made Jace's teeth ache. "I don't just like her. I love her."

Jace clenched his fists almost involuntarily, and Reid chuckled.

"What's the matter? Don't want Coop making a move on your friend?" He put air quotes around the last word.

"Douchebag."

"You're welcome."

Cooper cleared his throat. "Are you two going to stand around all day bickering like an old married couple or are we going to join the lady at the bar?"

"Join the lady." Jace turned his back on his friends and followed in Noelle's wake. He'd have to do a better job of hiding his emotions, that was for damn sure. He'd keep his promise to keep their relationship under wraps. But that didn't mean he was going to stand by and let Dumb or Dumber poach his girl from under his nose.

His girl. When the hell had that happened? And how?

He'd never been the possessive type. More of a don't-let-the-door-hit-you-on-the-way-out type.

But Noelle was different from the women he'd dated before. He'd known that going in. He just hadn't known she'd make him different, too.

"What'll it be, lover boy?" Reid bellied up to the bar a few feet away from Noelle, who'd struck up a conversation with an older couple in matching I Hiked the Grand Canyon T-shirts. "First round's on Coop."

Jace caught Noelle's eye and they exchanged a secret smile before he muscled his way in between his buddies. "If he's paying, I'll have a Glenfiddich. Neat."

Cooper laughed. "In this joint, you'll be lucky if they've got Dewar's White Label."

"Then make it a double. I'm not driving."

The previously silent jukebox roared to life and George Thorogood's "One Bourbon, One Scotch, One Beer" blared out. The crowd migrated to the dance floor.

"Great choice," Reid shouted over the music. Jace followed the first baseman's gaze to Noelle, who was signing a bar napkin for the Grand Canyon couple. Baseball might be America's pastime, but ballet apparently had its fans, too, even in copper country. "Maybe I'll ask your famous friend if she wants to join in on the fun with me."

"Do you even know how to line dance?"

Reid handed Jace his bourbon and took a sip from his own drink. "I'm a quick study."

Jace took a slug and thumped his glass down on the bar. "A little too quick, if you ask me."

"Do I have to separate you two again?" Cooper handed a pair of twenties over to the bartender. "Reid, stop needling Jace. And Jace, man up, admit you like the girl and ask her to dance. What are you afraid of? It's one song, not a lifetime commitment."

"Fine." Jace ran a hand through his hair and looked over at Noelle, who was engulfed in a bear hug from Mr. Grand Canyon. "Just don't make a big deal out of it."

"Seems like you're the one doing that." Cooper smirked and sipped his Pabst Blue Ribbon.

Jace couldn't disagree with him. Besides, the more he protested, the more his friends would suspect he and Noelle had already gone way past dancing. The best way to keep them in the dark was to shut up and play along.

Plus, he owed it to Noelle to rescue her from Huggy the Bear.

He strode over to the trio and laid a hand on Noelle's shoulder. Huggy reluctantly released her and stepped back.

"Sorry for the interruption." *Not.* Jace gave the couple what he hoped was his most charming smile. "But I believe the lady owes me a dance."

"I do?" Noelle looked up at him with eyes so blue and wide and innocent his gut clenched.

He was in trouble. Big trouble.

He shoved the unsettling feeling aside and bent to whisper in her ear, so close he could practically taste her grapefruit shampoo. "You do. Unless you'd rather stay and chew the fat with your geriatric groupies."

"Not nice," she hissed under her breath. But out loud she said, "That's right, I do."

Jace smiled into her hair.

Noelle straightened and addressed the couple. "I hope you don't mind."

"Of course not, dear." The older woman patted Noelle's arm reassuringly. "You've been more than generous with your time. Go dance with your young man."

"Oh, he's not…"

"Let's go, Duchess." Jace grabbed her hand and tugged her toward the dance floor. "The night is young, but it won't last forever."

12

NOELLE SAID A quick goodbye to the Kirbys, the lovely if demonstrative couple who had sold their Westchester home and were traveling across the United States in an RV. After a quick glance around the bar to make sure there weren't any other rabid fans with her or Jace in their sights, she let him lead her into the fray. "Take it easy on me. It's my first night out of the brace. And Sara says my knee's only eighty-five percent."

"Don't worry. I wouldn't want to anger the dragon lady."

Just as they found a square foot of free space on the dance floor, the music shifted to a slow number. Noelle hesitated, but Jace snaked an arm around her back and pulled her to him with authority, wedging a leg between hers and moving with the music. "Now they're playing our song."

"'Concrete Angel' is our song?" She pressed her lips together, fighting a smile.

"Is that what this is?"

"Kind of depressing, isn't it?"

Jace threaded his fingers through hers. With his other hand, he traced her spine from between her shoulder

blades to the dimples at the top of her butt, sending a now familiar tingling sensation straight to her girly parts. Even the most innocent touch and the damn man had her panties damp. So much for a certain Russian choreographer's theory that she was, in his words, *a frigid bitch*. Words he'd spat at her in front of the entire company.

She let herself relax, resting her head on Jace's warm, broad chest. He smelled of sandalwood and spearmint and his heart beat under her ear like a distant, steady drum, keeping time with the music. She half wished Yannick could see her now, in a dive bar, dancing to an overly sentimental Martina McBride tune he'd hate more than a badly executed tendu, in the arms of a guy he'd cross the street to avoid. He'd die of shock. Or laughter. Either way…

"I wasn't listening to the lyrics," Jace admitted, interrupting her thoughts. "Just digging the rhythm. Nice and slow. Perfect for this."

The hand at the small of her back pressed her to him. She gasped at the pressure of his erection against her thigh. Over his shoulder, she caught Cooper and Reid eying first her and Jace, then each other. "What will your friends think?"

"That I'm smart." Jace spun her around so her back was to the bar—and the boys. "And lucky."

"I don't know." She bit her lip. "Isn't PDA outside the scope of our agreement?"

"Look around. No one's paying a lick of attention to us. I'd be surprised if anyone other than your buddies Fred and Ethel even knows who either of us are."

Her eyes flitted from dancer to dancer. Jace had a point. Everyone else was too into the music or themselves or their partner to be bothering with yet another random couple who couldn't keep their hands off each other.

"Besides," Jace continued. "You can't leave me hanging out here."

"What do you mean?"

He rubbed against her, his erection digging into her thigh. "That's what I mean."

"And how is dirty dancing going to take care of your... problem?"

"It'll give me a few minutes to get it under control."

"What are you going to do?" She tipped her head to look him in the eye. "Wish it away?"

"It would help if you'd stop looking at me like that."

"Like what?"

"Like you haven't eaten in days and I'm a thick, juicy steak."

She shook her head and pushed back her hair. At the last minute, for reasons she didn't fully understand or want to, she'd opted to forgo her daytime ponytail and leave it down tonight for a softer, looser—dare she say sexier—look. "I prefer chicken. Less saturated fat and cholesterol."

"That's the ticket." He twined a finger in one of her curls that had fallen forward again, refusing to stay off her face. "Talk nerdy to me. The stock market. Black matter. Dr. Who."

She settled on what she thought was a nice, safe, if not particularly nerdy topic. "Your friends seem nice."

"They're okay, if you like arrogant, adolescent assholes."

"I like you, don't I?"

"I don't know, do you?"

Yeah, she did. They may have only known each other a few weeks, but their forced proximity meant she'd spent more time with him than she had with Yannick in months—outside work, of course. And she liked what

she'd seen. His easy, joking way with the staff at Spaulding. His weekly phone call to his father, who'd raised him pretty much single-handed. How he'd taken Dylan under his wing, working out with the teenager and patiently listening to endless baseball statistics and questions about every play-off game since the turn of the century. Not to mention all the trouble he'd gone through to take her to Fright Fest.

And therein lay the problem. There more she knew about Jace, the more she fell for him. There was a lot more to him than the womanizing, hotel-room-trashing image perpetuated by the tabloids.

And she ought to know better than most how wrong reporters could be.

But this wasn't supposed to be about falling for the guy. It was supposed to be about no-holds-barred, down-and-dirty sex with Mr. Right Now, not finding Mr. Right.

Then again, as her mother liked to say, sometimes it was easier to find something when you weren't looking for it.

"You're awfully quiet." Jace wound another finger into her hair and tucked the stray strands behind her ear. "Should I take that as a no?"

"No." She smiled at his puzzled expression. "I mean you shouldn't take it as a no. Not that my answer is no."

"So you do like me?"

Like and then some, but she was so not going there. Not now. Not ever.

"I don't make a habit of sleeping with men I don't like."

"Good to know."

He seemed satisfied with that answer, twining his fingers with hers and steering her around the floor. They danced in silence until the song ended and Big & Rich's

"Save a Horse (Ride a Cowboy)" took its place. Whooping and hollering, the dancing couples broke apart and lined up for the two-step. Noelle moved to join them, but Jace held her tightly to him.

"I think we're supposed to get in line for this one," she said.

But instead of releasing her, he lowered her into a dip, his face only inches from hers. "I've always been a rule breaker."

The movement of his lips so close to hers mesmerized her, and it took her a beat to respond. "You don't say?"

He hauled her up with a teasing laugh, breaking the spell. "Want the truth?"

"I don't know. You tell me."

"Once we leave this dance floor, I won't have a second alone with you until Cooper and Reid are out of our hair." He subtly maneuvered them to a quiet corner of the dance floor as he spoke. "Won't be able to touch you like this."

The hand on her back drifted down to cup her ass, squeezing.

"Or kiss you like this." He brushed his lips against her cheek in a way that should have felt chaste but didn't.

"Or do any the ten thousand other things I'm thinking of doing in public that would get me arrested. So forgive me if I'm not ready to let you go just yet."

"Oh." Had she said she was falling for him? Make that fallen, past tense. *Fait accompli.*

"That's all you've got?" Jace kissed her other cheek, then her jaw, then the corner of her mouth. "'Oh?'"

"You're lucky you got that." She clutched his shoulder for support as his lips slid to her neck. Much more and she'd melt into a puddle of lust at his feet. "I can't think when you do that."

"Do what?" he murmured against her throat. The vibrations rippled through her.

"You know what." She shuddered as his tongue stole out to taste the tender spot where her neck met her shoulder. "That."

"Duly noted." He tasted her again.

"We…we're going to have to stop dancing at some point. They're bound to call our table soon."

The words had barely left her mouth when the pager in her pocket buzzed. "Like now."

"Damn." He pulled back and looked down at her, his eyes sparking with mischief. "I was hoping that sound meant something else was in your pocket."

She wrinkled her nose and pulled out the flashing pager. "You're seriously warped."

"No." He gave her that sly, sexy smile that never failed to jump-start her heart. "Just eternally optimistic."

She gathered her wits enough to search over Jace's shoulder for Cooper and Reid. She found them chatting with a pair of scantily-clad redheads she guessed were sisters. "We'd better go rescue your friends."

Jace's eyes followed hers. "They don't look like they need rescuing. I say we finish out the song."

"The restaurant will give our table away."

He lifted a nonchalant shoulder. "There will be other tables."

"Face it, Prince Charming." She took his hand and dragged him past the two-steppers. "The clock's struck midnight and the party's over."

"If you say so, Cinderella." Jace went along without complaint. "But don't forget the rest of the story."

"You want me to lose a shoe so you can track me down?" She looked at her pink lace ballet flats with the suede trim that Holly had sent in response to Noelle's

desperate plea for some more of her clothes. Now that she'd gotten the all-clear to ditch the clunky brace, at least part-time, she could wear cute shoes again. No heels yet, of course. But at least they matched. "I'm kind of partial to these. They're Manolo Blahnik."

"Whatever that means." His smile made her pulse skitter. "But don't worry. You can hang on to your precious shoes. Both of them. I don't have to track you down. I know where you live, remember?"

"Then what?"

"The happy ending, babe," he whispered in her ear as they stopped in front of the hostess station. He took the pager out of her unprotesting hand, gave it to the woman behind the podium and motioned for his friends to join them. "It's all about the happy ending."

"I THINK I got one." Reid's line jerked. He stood, put his beer in the cup holder on the arm of his folding chair and plucked his pole from the sand.

"Are you sure it's a fish this time and not a tire?" Cooper taunted.

"That was an honest mistake." Reid waded a few inches into the water and planted his feet apart, slowly reeling in his line. "Damn thing weighed a ton and fought me every inch of the way."

"Just remember, we're aiming for striped bass, Professor. They're tastier than Goodyears. And a lot easier on the jaw."

Jace sat back and listened to his friends' good-natured bickering. They were always like this, the three of them. At each other constantly, but in a harmless, boys-will-be-boys kind of way. And when push came to shove, they had each other's backs. Night or day, no questions asked.

So what would his two best friends say now if they

knew their star shortstop, their fearless leader, the guy famous for his string of ballpark bunnies was hung up on a little bit of a ballerina with a whole lotta backbone and a big-ass attitude?

They'd only been at the lake a day and a half and he already missed her. Missed her like hell, with a palpable, physical ache. And he wasn't just talking about his neglected dick. He tried to tell himself it was because they hadn't had the chance to say a proper—translation, horizontal—goodbye before he took off with the infield idiots. But that was bullshit, and he knew it. He could screw her from now to eternity and it still wouldn't be enough. It would never be enough.

What scared him the most was that it wasn't just the sex he missed. It was *her*. Her perfume, a mix of fruit and flowers, lingering on his pillow. Her off-beat taste in music—something she called art punk, which she subjected him to during their joint workouts. The endearing habit she had of wishing on everything from dandelions to pennies to stray eyelashes.

Jesus Christ, he was turning into a major league pussy. He crushed the empty can in his fist and lobbed it into the cooler at his feet.

It's all about the happy ending. His syrupy sweet words echoed in his head. Had he actually said that to her? Who was he, Hans Christian Andersen?

This wasn't a fairy tale. Noelle had her life to go back to in New York. He had his in sunny California. And with three thousand miles in between, never the twain shall meet.

"Hey, Monroe," Cooper barked, snapping Jace out of his trance. "Think you can toss me a beer with that gimpy arm of yours? I'm gonna sit back, relax and watch the

Professor reel in the catch of the day. Or another hunk of rubber."

"My arm's fine," Jace lied, fishing a can from the cooler and making a show of aiming it with his trademark pinpoint accuracy into Cooper's waiting hands. But a beer can at twenty feet was one thing. A baseball across the diamond was another.

"I'm telling you, this one's dinner." Reid waded farther into the lake, the water seeping over the tops of his Wellingtons. The guy took his fishing seriously. He looked like he'd walked straight out of an Abercrombie & Fitch ad. "And you're cleaning it."

Ten minutes, a lot of splashing and a fair amount of swearing later, and Reid stood on dry land, proudly holding up a fat, shiny fish.

"Hope you've got your knife ready," he said, removing the hook from the fish's mouth, tossing his prize into a wire basket and handing the whole thing off to Cooper.

"You want to cook it inside or out?" the second baseman asked.

"Out." Reid wiped his hands on his pants and reached for his beer. "There's nothing like the taste of fresh fish grilled over a campfire."

Jace stood. "I'll go get some wood."

"I'll help." Reid finished his beer and threw the can into the cooler with the rest of the empties. "Then we can bring all this stuff back up to the campsite."

"Sounds like a plan." One-armed, Cooper folded up his chair. "I'll get started on the fish."

He headed for their campsite on Boulder Beach. Jace and Reid set off in the opposite direction. They hadn't gone ten feet when the interrogation began.

"So, now that we've gotten rid of the comic relief part of this trio, let's get serious. Tell me about your girl."

"Noelle." Jace bent to pick up some twigs for kindling. "Her name is Noelle."

"Her name's not important. What's important is that you're in love with her."

"You figured that out in less than twenty-four hours?" Jace kicked at a rock. "What are you, psychic?"

"I don't have to be. It's written all over you."

"How so?"

"Please. You were inches from flattening Coop just for staring at her ass a little too long. You're a textbook case, buddy boy."

"Of jealousy, maybe. That's a long way from love." Wasn't it?

"If you say so." Reid picked up a log. One end broke off in his hand, and he threw the rotted wood down. "But take it from me. Denial isn't just a river in Egypt."

A shadow flashed across Reid's face, so quick Jace almost missed it. What did he mean, take it from him? As long as Jace had known him, Reid had been a rolling stone, never sticking with one woman for long. Then again, the first baseman was notoriously close-mouthed about his private life. Even Jace and Cooper, his two closest friends, didn't know the story behind his scar.

Jace studied his friend but it was like staring at a blank wall. "Okay, let's say for the sake of argument that you're right. What am I supposed to do about it? We live on opposite coasts."

"You've heard of the Wright brothers. They invented this fancy flying machine called the aeroplane. I hear tell it can get you cross country in under five hours. Then there's texting, FaceTime, Skype…"

"I get the picture." Jace thought of his mother, waiting in some crappy, Double-A-salary apartment for his father to return from yet another extended road trip. Even if the

technology had existed back then, no amount of texting or Skyping or whatever-ing could have held that marriage together. "Long-distance relationships never work."

"Where there's a will, there's a way. If the girl's worth it." Reid pinned Jace with a look so pointed it made the hairs on the back of his neck stand on end. "Is she worth it?"

"What's with you, man?" Jace stopped midstride. This was super serious, even for the Professor. "You sound like Dr. Phil."

"Don't dodge the question. This is about your love life, not mine."

Jace didn't have to think long or hard to answer. "Yeah. She's worth it."

"Then take a risk. You're a power hitter, damn it. Swing for the fences."

"And if I strike out?"

"You won't."

"Psychic again?"

"Nah. Just observant. She could barely keep her eyes off you. She's as gone as you are. If you love her and let her go, you'll regret it. Trust me."

Again, Reid's face darkened, his scar seeming to become deeper, harsher, and Jace wondered exactly who had hurt him and how. But Reid didn't give him the chance to ask.

"We've got enough wood. Let's get back to camp."

Jace got the message. Subject closed. Not that he was complaining. They spent the rest of the time talking about safer stuff like the All-Star game and the Storm's chances in the play-offs.

"Took you guys long enough," Cooper scolded them when they finally made it to the campsite. "Jace, you

better check your phone. It's been blowing up for the past half hour."

Shit. He'd left his cell in the RV, not wanting to risk losing it in the lake. Service sucked outside the campground, anyway.

"Thanks."

He jerked open the door of the Airstream, panicked thoughts rushing his brain. His dad wasn't as young as he used to be. What if he'd fallen and hurt himself, or worse? Or maybe it was his agent, calling about his contract, which was due to expire at the end of the season.

And for the first time, a new concern cropped up to join the other, familiar ones: What if something had happened to Noelle?

Only one way to find out.

He dug his cell out from under a pile of *Field & Stream* magazines on the kitchen table that folded into the most uncomfortable bed he'd ever slept in—and he'd slept in some downright pitiful ones during his stint in the minors—and swiped the screen. Five missed calls, all from an unfamiliar number, and one voice mail.

He hesitated, then dialed, slumping against the table as he listened to the message.

"Dammit." He stabbed the end-call button with his finger and shoved the phone in his pocket.

"What's wrong?" Cooper asked.

"You look like shit," Reid, on his heels, added not so tactfully.

"I'm sorry, guys, but we have to cut this short." Jace scrubbed a hand across his jaw. "I've got to get back."

"To rehab?" Reid asked, all trace of smart-ass gone now. "Something up with Noelle?"

"To Sacramento." Jace's hands tightened into fists, his

fingernails digging into his palms. Painful, but it beat the alternative—punching a hole in the windshield. "It's my father. He's been arrested."

13

JACE HAD PLANNED to tell Noelle straight off. Maybe not all the gritty details about his father being behind bars, charged with gambling. Gambling, for Christ's sake. As worried as he was about his dad, he couldn't help but be a little pissed, too. What if he was betting on baseball? Or even worse, betting on—or against—the Storm? Did he want his son banned from the sport for life?

No, Jace wasn't confessing all of that to Noelle. He figured he'd be deliberately vague, tell her a family emergency meant he had to be on a plane home first thing tomorrow morning. Hopefully, she wouldn't fish for more information.

She'd been the first person he sought out when Cooper and Reid dropped him off at Spaulding. Just his luck, he'd tracked her down in the pool. One look at her slicing through the water, her lithe, slick body powerful and graceful and totally synchronized, and all his good intentions had flown out the window.

He waited until she reached the side of the pool closest to him and came up for air, gripping the edge with one hand and wiping the water out of her eyes with the other.

"Well, well." He smiled down at her, almost drowning

in the pleasantly-surprised look filling her baby blues. "Look what we have here. My very own mermaid."

"Jace." She blinked away a stray water droplet. "I thought you weren't due back until tomorrow."

"Would you believe me if I said I couldn't stay away?"

"From what?"

He squatted down in front of her and plucked a stray lock of wet hair off her face, letting his hand linger on her cheek. "From you. Mind if I join you?"

He stood and reached for the hem of his shirt.

"That depends." She crossed her arms on the edge of the pool, letting her legs float behind her. "Are you wearing a swimsuit under there?"

"Hell, no."

"Then come on in." She rested her chin on her forearms. "The water's fine."

Jace glanced at the door leading from the pool area to the locker rooms, then back at Noelle. "You're not afraid we'll get caught?"

She shook her head, spraying droplets all over the pool deck and onto his Vans. "It's after dinner. All the patients are back in their rooms, asleep or watching TV. Anyway, the pool's closed for the night. Sara told me to lock up when I'm done. So no one will be disturbing us."

Jace wasn't sure what had inspired the sudden attitude adjustment, but he wasn't about to question it. Not when she was wet and willing and—*holy crap*—peeling her swimsuit down over her perfect breasts.

"I figured if you're naked, I should be, too. I mean, what's good for the goose and all that, right?" She eyed his still-clad lower body. "You are going to get naked, aren't you?"

'Hell, yeah." He toed off his sneakers, shucked his

jeans and boxer briefs in one swift move and did a swan dive into the pool.

When he came up for air, he was a few feet behind her. She threw her swimsuit onto the deck next to his clothes and spun around to face him, using her elbows to brace herself on the ledge. "Are you crazy?"

"You're the one who invited me skinny-dipping."

"I meant diving. The water's not even six feet deep. You could have broken your neck."

"Worried about me, Duchess?" He swam up to her and took hold of the ledge on either side of her, trapping her between the side of the pool and his body. She felt soft and slick against his hardness as the lukewarm water gently lapped around them. "Be careful. I might start to think you have feelings for me."

"Of course I do. I told you, I don't sleep with men I don't like."

"'Like' is such a weak word. I like pizza. And beer. And watching stupid cat videos on YouTube." He punctuated each one with a kiss, tasting first her lips, then her throat, then those perfect breasts. "I'm talking about something a little deeper than that."

On the word *deeper*, he pushed a finger inside her, teasing her. She wrapped her legs around him and arched her back. After a few awkward thrusts, he withdrew and started walking to the shallow end of the pool.

"What are you doing?" She clutched at his shoulders, her nails digging into his back. The slight pain made the pleasure of her body sliding against his even more intense, and he had count to ten before he could answer.

"Deeper may be good for diving, but it's not so good for sex." He set her down on the pool steps and she lay back, propping herself up on her elbows. He leaned over her and plunged one finger into her again, then two, curv-

ing them to hit her G-spot. Her long, blond hair fanned out behind her and the water swirled around her hard, rosy nipples, making her look like a sexed-up mermaid. "See? Better, right?"

"Right," she panted, tipping her head back and closing her eyes. "So, so right."

"Open your eyes," he demanded. "I want to watch you when you come. I want you to watch me watching you, to see what you do to me."

Her eyes drifted open and she ground her hips against his hand in a wild, wide circle. Christ, she felt so good around him, like wet, smooth silk.

"I've never had sex in a pool before." Her cheeks flushed adorably, making his heart lurch.

"Technically, you're not now."

"Close enough," she said on a moan as a third finger joined the two already probing her center.

"Believe it or not, neither have I. Something we can both cross off our bucket list."

Even as he said it, he knew what they were doing was more than a checking off a box on a list. What they were doing might have started as two consenting adults scratching a sexual itch, but it had grown into something more than a friends-with-benefits fling. How much more, only time would tell.

Time they didn't have because he was leaving tomorrow morning.

He banished that thought and instead pushed into her with renewed urgency, any idea he might have had taking it slow and teasing her until she begged for release a speck in the rearview mirror. She seemed as desperate as he was, meeting him thrust for thrust, her nails raking tiny lines up and down his back.

The water sloshed over the lip of the pool onto the

tile as he drove her higher and higher. It didn't take long before she spiraled out of control, bucking and writhing until she was spent.

"Wow." Noelle flopped onto the step. "Now I know what I've been missing."

"Missing?" Jace splashed down next to her, then pulled her on top of him.

She tucked her head under his chin and sighed. "You know. The pool sex thing."

"Oh, that. I guess you do."

He felt her laugh rumble through him, and a pang of guilt stabbed him in the gut. "There's something I have to tell you. I…"

"Shhh." She put a finger to his mouth. "Not tonight. Whatever it is can wait until morning."

No, it couldn't.

"But…"

She added another finger and pressed them harder against his lips. "Please. I don't want anything to spoil this. Besides, I owe you one orgasm."

"It's not a contest."

"Tell that to Little Jace." She wriggled against his still hard dick. "Let's go back to my room. We can shower off the chlorine. I'll scrub your back. And your front."

Well, when she put it that way…

One more go-round wouldn't hurt. And it'd sure as hell make Little Jace happy. He could always tell her after they were showered and in her bed, in a state of postcoital bliss. Maybe it wouldn't sound so bad then.

"Okay." Jace stood, taking her with him, cradled against his chest. "But only if I can return the favor."

"JACE? ARE YOU AWAKE?" The form next to Noelle remained unmoving, the only sound coming from him a

soft snore. Not surprising given the workout they'd had, first in the pool, then the shower, then, finally, the bed.

With a soft sigh, she rolled gingerly to her side, not wanting to disturb him, and studied him in the half-light coming from the partially open bathroom door. He was beautiful, even in sleep. A lock of blue-black hair hung across his forehead. Dark lashes, sinfully long for a man, rested on his smooth, tanned cheeks like feathery fans. Stubble dotted his strong, square jaw.

And that was just his face.

The sheet had gathered around his waist, baring his thickly muscled chest and abs. Her fingers itched to pull it down a few inches and follow the trail of soft, fine hair to the treasure waiting at the end. She balled her hands into fists to resist the temptation. As much as she wanted to jump his bones for the fourth time that night, first she had to know what had really brought him back from his guys' weekend a day early.

"Jace?" she whispered again, nudging to his shoulder.

He opened his eyes. A grin that somehow managed to be both boyish and bawdy spread across his stubbled jaw. "Tired of staring at me?"

Heat infused her cheeks, and she said a silent prayer that the semidarkness hid her blush. "You were awake this whole time?"

"Not the whole time." He propped himself on his elbow and gazed down at her, his whiskey eyes flashing with amusement. "Just long enough to know you were enjoying the view."

Her face burned hotter. "A gentleman would have coughed or something."

"You should know by now, sweetness. I'm no gentle-man." He cupped her cheek, but she rolled away and sat

up, clutching the sheet around her bare breasts. "What time is it?"

She glanced at the clock on her nightstand. "Almost six."

"Good." He sat up next to her. "I have a couple more hours."

"A couple more hours until what?"

The boyish smile faded to a thin line. "We have to talk."

Right. He'd said there was something he had to tell her, but she'd distracted him with the promise of some sexy shower action. Whatever it was, she didn't want to hear it for some reason. She twisted the sheet in her fingers. "Is it the real reason you ditched your buddies and came back early?"

He stared down at his lap.

"I'm going home."

"You are?" She stared at him, her heart plummeting. He was leaving. She was staying. Whether she was ready or not, their little interlude was through. "That's...that's great. Then you've been cleared to play baseball again?"

"Not exactly." He threw off the sheet and stood.

She tried to ignore all the steel and sinew and concentrate on remembering to breathe and understanding what the hell he was saying. "What does that mean? Either you can play or not."

"Not." He bent to retrieve his boxers, giving her a choice view of his mouth-watering ass. "At least not yet. I've got some family business to attend to."

"Family business?"

He stepped into his boxers and sat next to her on the bed, stroking her leg through the sheet. "Nothing for you to worry about."

She shoved his hand away. The sheet slipped below

one breast and she scrambled to cover herself. "Don't patronize me."

He ran his fingers through his sleep-rumpled hair. "What do you want me to do?"

"I want you to be honest with me."

"It's not pretty." He caressed her cheek with his thumb.

She leaned into his touch. "I'm tougher than you think. I can handle ugly."

"I know you can, Duchess." His gaze dropped to her mouth and his thumb shifted from her cheek to graze her lower lip. "But you shouldn't have to handle my ugly."

"I want your ugly." She turned her head to kiss his palm, then took his hand in hers. "Even if it's the last thing you share with me."

He opened his mouth, and for a second she thought he was going to contradict her, tell her this wouldn't be their last moment together, that they'd make it work three thousand miles apart. But then he pressed his lips together and took a shallow breath. After what seemed like an eternity, he spoke, his voice uncharacteristically flat. "It's my father. He's in jail."

"He's what?" She couldn't have heard that right. From all Jace had told her about his hard-working, blue-collar, single dad, jail seemed like the least likely place for him to be.

"Something about gambling. I don't have all the details yet. But I've got to get home ASAP so I can bail him out and hire an attorney. My flight leaves in a few hours. Guess I'd better get packing."

He stood and picked up his pants and shirt from the floor where they'd landed the night before, only seconds after the door closed behind him.

"What about your rehab?"

"Sara's already agreed to forward my records to the

team doc. He'll set something up closer to home. It won't be Spaulding, but I'll make it work."

She didn't doubt that. He approached his recovery with razor-sharp focus and single-minded determination. The same way he'd pursued her.

"I'll go with you to the airport." Still wrapped in the sheet, she shuffled awkwardly over to her bureau and rifled through the drawers for clean underwear and something halfway presentable to wear.

"Better not." He pulled his pants over lean hips. "I hate tearful goodbyes. And we wouldn't want to make a big, dramatic scene at the terminal, where anyone could snap a pic on their cell phone and sell it to the tabloids."

She dangled a black lace demi cup bra from her fingers, frowned and shoved it back in the drawer, opting instead for a more demure but still attractive number in seafoam green satin that covered a lot more real estate. No use dressing for sex when she wasn't going to get any. "I didn't think you cared about that stuff."

"No." He zipped his fly and shrugged on his shirt. "But you do."

Something inside her melted. He might be leaving, but that didn't mean he didn't care about her, at least a little. Enough to make sure she didn't risk her reputation by making a fool out of herself in public.

But not enough to take their fling to the next level.

She hip-checked the drawer closed. "Well, if you're sure…"

He slipped his feet into his Vans and strode over to her, cupping her face in his hands. "I've never been less sure about anything. But something tells me it'll hurt less if we do this quick, like stealing second."

Her heart latched onto his admission that leaving would hurt. It was a thin thread of hope she could cling

to when she was lying alone in her bed at Spaulding, something she hadn't done much of since they'd first hooked up. "Will you call and let me know you got there in one piece?"

He kissed her. Long and lingering, like he was savoring one last taste. When he was done, he stepped back and thrust his hands in his pockets. "I'll try. Things are going to be kind of crazy with my dad."

"It's okay. I understand." She did. She really did. His father had to be his priority right now. And what they'd had was only temporary. She'd known that from the start. Not that any of that made his sudden departure any easier. "I hope everything works out."

He crossed back to her and kissed her again, hard and fast this time, putting a period on their relationship. "So do I, Duchess. So do I."

She watched him turn and go, the door swinging shut behind him, clicking closed with a finality that echoed the emptiness in her chest.

14

"HERE." JACE SET a bowl down in front of his father. "My specialty. Chicken noodle soup. From a can."

"Thanks."

Jace leaned against the counter and watched his father slurp his soup. Nothing much had changed since he'd been at his dad's place last. No new refrigerator. No drainage system. No sump pump.

Of course, now Jace knew where all the money he'd been sending had really gone—into the pocket of one Light Fingers Lenny. The guy was the biggest bookie in the greater Sacramento area, and the authorities wanted his father to testify against him in exchange for a reduced sentence.

"Don't thank me yet. You haven't heard what it's going to cost you." Jace grabbed a Rolling Rock out of the refrigerator, popped the top off and took a seat across the table from him.

His father laid his spoon down. "Cost me?"

"When you're done eating, we're going to talk."

"Didn't we do that a few hours ago at the police station?"

Jace took a swig, grimaced and thunked the beer bot-

tle down on the table. "I don't want the crap you gave your lawyer. I don't care about the where or the when or the how. I want to know why. Why the hell were you gambling? Did you need money? Were you betting on baseball? Please tell me you weren't betting on baseball."

"That's a lot of questions."

"I need some answers, Dad. Were you betting on the Storm?"

"No." His father slumped in his seat. "I didn't bet on the Storm or any other baseball team. I'd never do anything to jeopardize your career. You know that."

"I don't know anything anymore." Jace clenched and unclenched his fists under the table. "Why, Dad? I would have given you whatever you needed."

His father seemed to slump even further. "A man's supposed to support his son, not the other way around."

Jace didn't bother to point out that he'd been supporting his father bit by bit for years. No use kicking him when he was down, no matter how pissed off Jace was. "You supported me for eighteen years. All by yourself, I might add. What's the big deal if the tables are turned now?"

"It wasn't about the money. At least not at first."

"Then what was it about?"

"Having something to do with my days. Not being bored out of my ever-loving skull. So when the guys asked me to go to the track…" His father's voice trailed off and he tugged at his ear, a sure sign Jace was treading into dangerous—or at least uncomfortable—territory. "It just kind of snowballed from there."

"What do you mean, bored? You've got the repair shop to keep you busy."

"I haven't wanted to tell you, but business has been dropping off steadily for the past year or two. Half the

time things aren't worth fixing. Everything is disposable. It's cheaper to buy something new. And the other half of the time I'm dealing with newfangled electronics that are so complicated, I couldn't fix them if I wanted to." His father let out a heavy sigh and buried his head in his hands. "I'm a dinosaur, Jace. A relic of a bygone era."

"What about the Wurlitzer?"

"Done. And it was the only project I've had in the last two months, except for fixing Mrs. Robertson's ancient toaster that she refuses to part with."

Jace's wanted to kick himself into next week. This was his father. How could he not have known he was struggling? He was too obsessed with his own damned career, too busy getting wasted and chasing tail, that was how. He was glad his father's head was down, because he couldn't look him in the eye. "You should have told me."

"Pretty damn humiliating, admitting to your offspring that you're a failure."

"You're not a failure, Dad." Jace ran a finger around the lip of his beer bottle. "And I'm not Mom."

"I'm well aware of that."

"Are you?" Jace leaned back in his chair and sipped his beer. "You raised me. Fed me. Clothed me. Got me to practice on time. And God knows, I was no angel. I'm not going to abandon you just because you fell on hard times or made a few mistakes."

"More than a few." His dad picked up his spoon, swirled it around in what remained of his now room temperature soup, then let it clatter back down on the table. "I'm sorry, son. I should have come to you when it got out of hand. Then I wouldn't have had to run bets for Lenny to pay off my debt."

"You should have come to me before it got out of hand. But it's okay." Jace backpedaled at the stricken look on

his father's face, reaching across the table to cover his father's hand—more wrinkled than Jace remembered. "I'm here now. We'll get this fixed. Like the DA said, you'll testify against Lenny, plead to a lesser offense and get probation."

"Will I have to move?" His father pulled his hand away. "Lenny's got a lot of friends. Dangerous ones. They're not gonna be too happy with me if I help put him behind bars."

"Maybe," Jace admitted, figuring it was better to be honest from the get-go. That way his dad could start mentally preparing himself for the possibility that he might have to relocate, maybe even go into witness protection. Jace didn't even want to think about the complications. "But we'll jump off that bridge when we come to it."

His poor attempt at humor was rewarded with a wry chuckle.

"You're a good kid, Jace. A good man," his father corrected, pushing back his chair, picking up his still half-full bowl and carrying it to the sink.

Good? Jace wasn't so sure about that. And his father would probably think differently, too, if he read the tabloids.

"If I am, it's because of you." He polished off his beer and grabbed two more from the fridge. Popping off the tops, he offered one to his father and checked the clock on the stove. "The Storm's playing Milwaukee in ten. Wanna watch?"

His father took the bottle and drank. "It doesn't bother you, watching the team while you're on the sidelines?"

"Nah." Jace hoped to hell the lie sounded convincing. Bothered was a mild word for what he felt about that wet-behind-the-ears pissant Hafler in his place at short, lighting it up at the plate and in the field. But the best way to

beat the competition was to know them inside out, and that meant studying Hafler's every move so he'd be ready to take him on in spring training.

"Come on." Jace slung his good arm around his father's shoulder. "Let's watch on the big screen in the den. We can order some pizza."

"Are pizza and beer on your rehab diet?" His father's graying brows knotted. "I wouldn't want you to go against doctor's orders. Bad enough I dragged you away from that swanky center the Storm sent you to."

"It won't hurt me to indulge a little." Jace steered his dad out of the kitchen and down the hall to the den. "And I'm meeting with the team physician next week to talk about transitioning my treatment to an out-patient facility in Sacramento."

"You mean you're not going back?" His father stopped short in the middle of the hallway, and Jace had to do the same to avoid crashing into him. "I thought once..."

"You thought wrong. It's okay, Dad," Jace reassured him. "I can finish up my rehab just fine here. And you and I can spend some real time together for a change."

Both were true, to an extent. The team would hook him up with some perfectly acceptable facility. And he did want to see his father more, help him sort through not just this legal mess but his business problems, too. Maybe he'd even stay with his dad for a while.

But even more true was the fact that Jace couldn't go back to Spaulding given the way he'd left things with Noelle. Hell, he hadn't even contacted her since he'd left except for a brief text letting her know he was home safe, which she'd acknowledged with an equally brief *thanks*. It wouldn't be fair to her to show up on her doorstep expecting to pick up where they'd left off. Unless he had something more to offer her. Like commitment...

"What is it?" His father ran a hand through his salt-and-pepper hair. "There's something you're not telling me."

"The game's about to start." Changing the subject was a legitimate avoidance strategy, wasn't it? Jace clapped his father on the shoulder and continued down the hall into the den. "What do you want on your pizza?"

His father followed him. "Your arm's worse than you're letting on, isn't it? Or my case isn't as open-and-shut as you're leading me to believe."

"It's nothing like that. I swear." Jace sank into the nut-brown butter-leather sectional he'd bought his dad last Christmas and hunted for the TV remote.

"Well, if it's not baseball and it's not my legal troubles, there's only one thing it can be." His father sat next to him, giving him the same penetrating look he'd given him as a seven-year-old when Jace had taken a permanent marker to his dad's prize possession—a baseball signed by Brooklyn Dodger ace Sandy Koufax. "A woman."

Looked like full-on denial was up to bat next. Hadn't worked all that well with the Koufax ball, but it was all Jace had left up his sleeve. Bad enough Cooper and Reid knew about Noelle. No way was he discussing his love life with his father.

"Just one?" Jace propped his feet up on the coffee table, trying to project *ladies' man* and not *big fat liar*. "Not likely."

"Fine. I understand. Don't want to talk about it with your old man. Can't say I blame you, given my track record with the fairer sex. But if you don't mind one piece of advice…"

Jace shrugged and sipped his beer. "Shoot."

"Women aren't mind readers, as much as they'd like

us to think they are. If you love her, tell her. Don't wait until it's too late."

"Was that what happened with Mom?" They'd never really talked much about her. Jace had only been five when she'd left without looking back, right about the time his dad had quit playing ball after toiling for years in the minors. He'd always assumed the two were connected. But maybe there was more to the story.

"I'm not sure." His father took a long, slow pull of his beer, his forehead wrinkled in concentration. "Your mother was never really happy as the wife of a small-time ballplayer. And she wasn't exactly thrilled with the idea of me as a handyman. But I'm not the most demonstrative guy. Maybe if I had paid more attention to her, been a little more affectionate...who knows?"

Jace knew. He'd tried being the perfect son—quiet, neat, obedient—thinking it would put a smile on his mother's face for a change. It hadn't worked. And nothing his dad could have done would have kept her from bailing on them, either.

But his father had a point. Jace had up and left Noelle hundreds of miles away without manning up and admitting that, when it came down to it, he didn't want their relationship to have a time stamp. He wasn't ready to call it love, but he wasn't ready to call it quits, either.

Now he just needed to figure out how to make things right with her.

"Thanks, Dad." Jace found the remote stuck between the couch cushions and hit the power button, flicking through the channels to find the game. "I'll take it under advisement."

"Good." His father kicked his feet up onto the table next to Jace's. "Now about that pizza..."

"ARE YOU READY for this?" Sara asked, plunking herself down on the exercise bench across from Noelle.

"Shouldn't you know the answer to that?" Noelle half joked. It was the first time she'd felt even remotely like laughing or smiling in the weeks since Jace left. But the next few minutes had the potential to improve her mood dramatically. "You're the physical therapist."

"You're ready. You've been a model patient. Your rehab's progressing right on schedule. I don't make guarantees, but I'll be surprised if Dr. Sun doesn't clear you for the next phase of your treatment."

"The next phase?"

"Phase four. Focusing on technique, power and performance by practicing sport-specific movements and tasks."

"Speak English, not therapist."

"If he gives the thumbs-up, you're going back to New York to start dancing again."

Noelle squealed. "You're serious?"

"Down, girl." Sara put a hand on her good knee. "Dr. Sun has to approve. And we're talking baby steps. Pliés at the barre, not pirouettes across the floor."

"I'm impressed you know what either of those are."

Sara laughed. "It would have been impossible to spend all these weeks working with you and not pick up a little ballet terminology."

"Ladies." A distinguished looking man in what looked to be his midseventies poked his head through the door. Dr. Sun, Noelle presumed. He confirmed it a second later when he introduced himself and held out his hand to her. "And you must be Miss Nelson."

"Noelle," she corrected him, taking his hand and shaking it.

"Shall we get started?"

"Of course." She stood. "The sooner the better."

For the next half hour, he took her through a series of range-of-motion and strength-training exercises, grunting and scribbling in her chart after each set, not once revealing what he was thinking.

"Good, good," he murmured finally.

"So I can dance?" Noelle took the water bottle Sara offered her, popped the top and drank.

"One more test." Dr. Sun patted one of the exercise benches. "Lie on your back with your heel resting on the edge."

She did as he asked, and he flexed her knee.

When he was done, Noelle sat up. "What's the verdict, doc? Was leaving my family and friends and trekking more than halfway across the country worth it?"

"If by worth it you mean did coming here get you healed and healthy as fast as possible, then yes. You're cleared to dance." He held up a cautionary hand, palm out. "You'll have to start slowly, of course. Basic, simple moves only. I'll be sending your file to the company doctor in New York, and Sara will be consulting with your physical therapist there to make sure you stay on track."

"Oh, I will, I promise. Thank you, Dr. Sun." Noelle jumped up and hugged the surprised doctor then turned to her therapist, arms open. "And you, too, Sara. I couldn't have done this without you."

Sara returned the hug. "I don't know about that. You're one of the most motivated patients I've ever worked with. But if you're offering it up, I'll gladly take the credit for your success."

Noelle gave Sara a quick squeeze before releasing her, and the two women said their goodbyes to Dr. Sun. When he was gone, Noelle sank back down onto the bench, still in a state of happy shock. Sure, she had a long way

to go yet. It'd be months before she was strong enough
to perform in front of an audience. But she was going
to dance again. The career she'd worked so hard for was
back within her grasp, so close she could taste it. "What
happens next?"

"I'll have the front office make arrangements for you
to fly out as soon as possible." Sara sat next to her. "I
know I'm not supposed to say this, but I think I'll miss
you most of all, Scarecrow."

"Thanks. I'll miss you, too." Noelle reached under the
bench for her water bottle, suddenly itching to get back
to her room, where she'd left her cell phone charging on
the nightstand. News like this was too good not to share.
She had to tell…

Jace.

Excitement traded places with regret, which settled on
her like a cold, wet blanket. Jace was the one person she
most wanted to talk to now, the one person who would
best understand what it meant to be given your liveli-
hood—no, your dream, your life, your goal since you
could walk—back again.

Unfortunately, he was also the person who hadn't
bothered to communicate with her in the more than two
weeks since his abrupt departure, save for one two-word
text letting her know he'd arrived safely in Sacramento.
And, okay, her response had been just as brief. But she
had been following his lead. It was obvious he didn't want
anything more to do with her. Wasn't it?

"Hey." Sara tapped Noelle's shoulder to get her attention. "Where'd you go? This is supposed to be good
news, and you look like your man dumped you, your
truck broke down and your dog died."

"It is good news. It's just…" Noelle stopped herself.
The one drawback of keeping whatever it was she'd been

doing with Jace quiet was that she had no one to confide in. Not even her sisters knew she'd broken down and slept with him. And slept with him. And slept with him. And…

"Ohmigod, it's Jace, isn't it?" Sara eyes went wide. "You wish he was still here so you could share this with him."

Crappity crap crap crap. Noelle wondered what had given her away. Probably the Cheshire cat look on her face when she thought about sex with Jace. Maybe it wasn't too late to bail herself out. "That's not…"

Sara cut her off with a wave. "Don't bother denying it. The whole staff's been buzzing about you two."

"What?"

"Well, maybe not the whole staff. Just the ones with eyes. And ears. And half a brain."

"Great." Looked like they hadn't fooled anyone. Noelle let her head fall into her hands and groaned. "Just what I wanted. My love life the hot topic at the water cooler."

Again.

"Don't worry." Sara gave Noelle's arm a reassuring pat. "We may not be blind, deaf or dumb, but we can be discreet. And if it counts for anything, consensus is you guys make a great couple."

"You mean made."

"No, I mean make." The pat turned into a squeeze. "You balance each other out. He makes you…I don't know…lighter. Less serious. And I probably shouldn't be telling you this—you know, patient confidentiality and all—but he was way easier to work with after you two hooked up. Even followed my directions…most of the time."

Sara rolled her eyes.

"We left things sort of…" Noelle waved a hand ab-

sently "…up in the air. And he hasn't called or texted since the day he left."

"So? You've got dialing fingers. Call him."

"I don't know…"

"Don't know what?" Sara smacked the arm she'd been squeezing. "Get with the program. This is the twenty-first century, girlfriend. Take the initiative. Your future is in your hands. Female empowerment and all that jazz."

"Thanks. I'll think about it." Noelle got up. "I'm going for a swim."

"Good idea." Sara rose, joining her. "You can work out the kinks in your knee. And your head."

Exactly what Noelle was hoping. Thirty minutes in the pool had a way of loosening up not just her muscles but her mind. Maybe she'd figure out some way to have her career and her man, too.

If that's even what he wants, a little voice deep inside her whispered. She squashed it down and crossed to the door. When she reached it, she turned back to Sara. "I meant what I said before. I owe you, big time."

"Go." Sara shooed her away. "Before this gets all sappy and sentimental. And neither of us wants that."

Less than fifteen minutes later, Noelle was in her swimsuit and in the pool. Breaststroke, backstroke, butterfly, freestyle. A childhood spent swimming in Long Island Sound had taught her well, and now she worked her way through them all in methodical order, switching every third lap. With each length of the pool, her knee felt better, stronger, more stable.

Unfortunately, the same couldn't be said for her muddled brain. Twenty laps and she was no closer to solving the Jace dilemma. Her mind kept drifting back to the night he'd found her swimming and given her one of the best orgasms of her life with only his fingers.

Sputtering, she stopped midlap and floated on her back. Sara was right. There was no way around it. If she wanted him—and she did—she was going to have to go out on a limb and pick up the phone. After all, what was the worst that could happen? Flat-out rejection? Utter humiliation? Been there, survived that, thanks to Yannick.

Although something told her it'd be worse this time around if Jace was the one doing the rejecting. What she'd felt for Yannick was a schoolgirl crush. What she felt for Jace was…different. Bigger. Maybe even big enough to be—dare she say—love. And the bigger the love, the harder the fall. Still, it was a risk she had to take if she wanted the reward.

And she wanted it. Bad.

Mind made up, Noelle hauled herself out of the pool. A quick shower later, she was on her bed, staring at the cell phone in her hand like it was a live grenade.

Sara's words echoed in her head. *Twenty-first century. Take the initiative. In your hands. Female empowerment.*

Before she could change her mind, Noelle pulled Jace's name up in her contacts list and hit Talk.

15

THERE WAS NOTHING quite like waking up to the strains of "Welcome to the Jungle," played through the tinny speakers of a cell phone.

"Hang on," Jace muttered to no one as he groped, eyes still closed, on the nightstand for his phone. After a few seconds of fruitless searching and a disturbing thud that told him he'd knocked something over, he cracked one eye open and spied the offending device on the floor next to the bed, still ringing and apparently unharmed.

"'Lo?" he answered, his voice gravelly and his words slurred as if he'd been sleeping. Which, of course, he had been. What the hell time was it?

He opened his other eye to get a good look at the bed-side clock. Barely 8:00 a.m. No civilized person would dare call at that hour without a damn good reason. Which meant, whoever it was, odds were it wasn't good news.

"Hello?" he repeated, slightly more articulate this time now that he was starting to join the land of the living. "Anybody there?"

"Ohmigod, did I wake you?" a familiar female voice came across the line. "Crap. I forgot about the time dif-ference. I'll call back later."

"Noelle. Don't hang up." He was fully awake now, and he struggled to sit. If he'd been more alert, he'd have seen her name on his caller ID. "I take it you got my package."

"Your what?"

"I sent you a care package." He'd wanted to reach out to her with more than a simple phone call.

"Like the one your buddies sent you?" He could almost picture her arching one perfectly tweezed brow.

"Not quite." He chuckled. "So if you haven't gotten my little surprise yet, to what do I owe the pleasure of this phone call?"

"It's a pleasure?"

His gut twisted at the uncertainty in her voice. His fault, he knew. "Of course. Why wouldn't it be?"

"I wasn't sure. The way you left…and then your text…"

She trailed off, sounding a bit like a jilted lover. Which she was, thanks to him. But that didn't mean he wanted her to sound like one. Or stay one.

"Yeah, about that." He paused, not exactly sure what he was going to say. He was walking a tightrope, trying to balance on a thin wire with love and commitment on one side and his hard-drinking, hard-partying, man-whore days on the other. "My life is…complicated right now. But I'd like it if we could be…"

"Friends?"

He stretched and scratched his stomach. "I was hoping for a little bit more than that."

"Friends with benefits, then?" she suggested.

He grimaced. He'd never minded the expression before. But he sure as hell minded it now. It was too small, too crude for what he had—or wanted to have—with Noelle. "Do we have to put a label on it?"

"No," she said after a long minute during which their

entire relationship flashed before his eyes. Her falling through the therapy room door. Walking in on him with that damned blowup doll. Practically jumping into his lap at Fright Fest. And then there was the sex…

"We're both adults," she continued, interrupting his erotic daydream. "We know the score."

"Good." He breathed a relieved sigh and leaned back against his pillow. "Now that we've got that settled, why don't you tell me what prompted this call?"

"Do I need a reason?"

"No." He crossed his arms behind his head. "But knowing you, you've got one."

"I do. I'm going home."

In an instant, the few hundred miles between them became a few thousand. Still, he couldn't help the admiration for her that swelled his chest. She'd worked her ass off and now she was reaping the reward. "So they're letting you hit the dance floor again?"

"Only baby steps at first, but…"

"No buts." Jace ran a hand through his hair. Christ, he wished he was back at Spaulding so he could take her in his arms and kiss her until they were both out of breath and out of their minds with lust. "That's fantastic. I knew you could do it."

"That makes one of us."

He couldn't tell whether she was joking or not. "Seriously. You'll be doing those fancy turns across the stage in no time."

She laughed. "I think you mean fouettés."

"You're the expert." He flung off the covers, leaving him naked as the day he was born. He imagined her expression if she could see him now. An instant of shock, quickly morphing into glassy-eyed desire. Too bad they weren't on Skype. "When do you leave for New York?"

"I'm not sure. Tomorrow, probably. The front office is taking care of it."

Damn. No time for a quick trip to the desert. He'd have to wait until things with his father were settled before he could see her in the Big Apple. He swung his legs over the side of the bed and reached for a pair of boxers in the pile of—he hoped—clean clothes on the floor. "You'd better get packing then. Promise you'll call when you get there."

"Will do."

"And let me know when you get my package."

"What if I'm gone by the time it gets here?"

"Don't worry." He pulled his boxers on over his morning wood and stood, scratching his stomach again. "I'm sure they'll forward it to you."

"What is it? Can't you at least give me a hint?"

"And ruin the surprise?" He clucked his tongue. "Fat chance. You'll just have to wait."

"Spoilsport."

"I prefer to think of it as heightening the anticipation. You know what they say. Good things come to those who wait."

He sure as hell hoped so. Because it looked like he was going to have to wait awhile longer for the best part of getting back together—make-up sex.

"She's here! Elena, she's here!"

Her father's voice boomed from the porch of the Nelson family homestead as Noelle climbed out of her Mini Cooper. Within seconds, her mother, brother, sisters and their respective spouses spilled out into the gravel driveway to greet her.

You'd think she'd been gone two years instead of two months.

"Come inside," her mother more ordered than re-

quested after everyone had doled out hugs, kisses and, in Cade's case, noogies. "I made rigatoni bolognese. And *insalata caprese* to start. Your favorites, *passerotta*."

Little sparrow. Her mother's nickname for her. She said Noelle went straight from crawling to dancing, flitting from place to place like a bird.

"Everything you make is my favorite, Ma." Not that she could eat much of it. Her mother's idea of a balanced meal was carbs, carbs and more carbs, with a little protein on the side.

Sunday dinner was a tradition at the Nelsons, but it had been a while since the whole family sat down at the table together. Between Holly's newfound success as a playwright, Gabe's duties as Manhattan's District Attorney, Ivy's growing photography business and Noelle's performance schedule, at least one of them was usually missing in action.

"To what do we owe this rare pleasure?" Noelle asked, pulling out a chair at the big oak table that dominated the farmhouse kitchen. "All six Nelsons in the same hemisphere. And it's not even a holiday."

"Are you kidding?" Gabe plunked himself down in the chair opposite her, elbows on the table. "I wouldn't miss this for the world."

"Miss what?" Noelle asked.

Nick sat next to Gabe with a smirk. "The grilling you're going to get from Holly and Ivy."

"What's there to grill me about?" As if she didn't know.

"Jace Monroe," Nick answered. "Your new boy toy."

"Traitor," Holly muttered, giving her husband a not-so-subtle smack upside the head as she took the seat on his other side.

"Yeah," Ivy said, joining them at the table with Cade,

who settled in beside her. "We were going to wait until after dinner. At least let her enjoy her rigatoni."

"What little of it she'll eat," Holly added.

"Don't you have a baby to take care of?" Noelle reached for a piece of bread from the basket at the center of the table. The carbs would be worth it. If she had her mouth full, she couldn't be expected to answer questions.

"Joy's upstairs, napping in her Pack 'n Play," Holly said. "Which means I've got about forty-five minutes. Let the third degree begin."

"Don't worry," Gabe's fiancée, Devin, assured her best friend. "If she wakes up before then I'll take care of her. I could use the practice. Who knows? We could be next."

She sat next to Gabe and they exchanged a look so full of love and tenderness, it made Noelle want to jump on a plane to Sacramento. She and Jace had been texting and calling and Skyping daily in the week or so since her first phone call, but none of that, no matter how steamy, was a match for up-close-and-personal, longing looks.

Instead, she had to put on her game face and stand up to an interrogation the likes of which only the Nelsons could muster. The Spanish inquisitors had nothing on her siblings.

"*Mangia e statti zitto.*" Noelle's mother slapped a platter of fresh mozzarella, tomato and basil salad on the table. "Stop your bickering and eat. There will be plenty of time to ask Noelle all the questions you want after dessert."

Her parents took their traditional seats at opposite ends of the table, and the rest of the meal progressed as peacefully as a Nelson Sunday dinner could. Until the second the last dessert plate hit the dishwasher, and her sisters and sister-in-law let the questions fly.

"Ok, spill. What's the deal with this Jace guy?"

"Is he as hot as he looks on TV?"

"Did you two do the deed?"

Noelle shot a glance at her parents, still seated at the table sipping their coffee, then glared at her siblings. "I am so not talking about this in front of the parental units."

"*Tack så mycket.*" Nils Nelson shuddered. "Thank you. There are some things a father doesn't need to know about his little girl."

"Noelle's right." Holly closed the dishwasher and hit the start button, the machine's low hum underscoring her words. "Come on, ladies. Let's take a walk. We can finish this discussion in the greenhouse."

"Discussion?" Noelle wiped her hands on a dishtowel and draped it over the edge of the sink. "Is that what we're calling it?"

"What about us dudes?" Gabe asked, leaning back in his chair. "We'll miss all the fun."

"Yeah," Nick chimed in. "Now who's the traitor?"

"Don't worry, babe. I'll fill you in later." Holly came up behind him and dropped a kiss on the top of his head. "Can you check on Joy? She should be waking up soon."

"No sweat." Nick reached back and squeezed his wife's hand. "Go have your girl talk. I'll take care of the baby."

Another pang of longing—or was it jealousy?—hit Noelle. She wanted what her brother and sisters had. She wanted a home, and someone to share it with.

Could Jace be that someone?

For so many years her career had consumed her life, taken up every waking moment, every inch of free space. Where she went, who she knew, what she ate were all dictated by ballet. The only person she'd dared to imagine a future with was Yannick, and that was only because he was already a part of that world.

Jace was about as far from Yannick as a fish was from a bicycle. Yet the more she thought about it, the more she realized she and Jace made sense together in a way she and Yannick never had. They just…fit. He was the light to her dark, the yin to her yang, the Rudolf Nureyev to her Margot Fonteyn. Sure, it would be a challenge juggling their respective careers. But a career couldn't keep her warm at night.

Or give her multiple orgasms.

"Earth to Noelle." Ivy snapped her fingers in her sister's face. "Greenhouse. Stat."

"Fine." Noelle pushed off the counter and followed the others. She might as well get it over with. They were going to wring the dirty details out of her sooner or later. Maybe when they were done with their good-natured prying, they'd have some words of wisdom for her.

"Okay," she said when the greenhouse door had closed behind the last of them and the thick, musky scent of her father's prize roses wafted around her. "Let me have it."

"Are we that bad?" Holly asked, overturning a five-gallon bucket and sitting on it.

"Yes, you are." Devin sat cross-legged on the floor beside her. "But I survived. Barely."

"Cut us some slack." Ivy pulled up a garden stool and plopped herself down. "We're just excited to see you with someone other than Yakov."

"Yannick." Noelle looked around for something to sit on and came up short. She settled for widening her stance, hands on her hips. "And who says I'm *with* anyone."

Ivy blew out an exasperated raspberry. "The shining eyes. The rosy cheeks. The way you keep checking your cell phone every other minute."

"And smiling every time you get a text," Holly added.

"Ooh, are you sexting?" Devin licked her lips. "Can we read them?"

Noelle stamped her foot. "Absolutely not."

"You're absolutely not sexting, or we absolutely can't read them?" Devin asked with a smirk.

"Focus, ladies, focus," Holly, clearly the ringleader, scolded, then turned her attention to Noelle. "In all seriousness, baby sister, we just want to let you know we're happy for you. And if you need anything, like advice on how to balance two demanding careers…"

"Or some sexy boudoir photos to remind him how good he's got it when he's on the road… " Ivy offered.

"Or a tasteful tattoo as a symbol of your love, in a discreet location, of course…" This from Devin.

"We're here for you," Holly finished.

Noelle's gaze bounced from sister, to sister, to sister-in-law, her eyes growing increasingly moist. Her family really was the best, even if she occasionally wanted to exile them to a deserted island. She blinked the tears away and broached the subject she was most interested in. "Well, there is one thing."

"The pictures?" Ivy asked.

"The tattoo?" Devin suggested.

"Generous offers, both, but no." Noelle smiled. "At least not now. What I'm curious about is how did you all know?"

"Know what?" Holly sat forward, elbows on her knees, if possible even more intent.

Noelle took a deep breath and plowed on, knowing once she said the words, there was no going back. "That you'd found the one person you were meant to be with for the rest of your life."

"Christ." Devin released her long, dark hair from the

clip that had been holding it back. "When you put it that way, it sounds so…"

"Ridiculous?" Noelle sank to the stone floor next to her sister-in-law.

"No." Devin shook her head, sending her newly freed tresses flying. "Impossible. Like finding a polar bear in a snowstorm. Yet here we are, Holly, Ivy and me. Living proof it's not."

"I knew with Cade when he brought me fire safety equipment after I almost burned down Holly and Nick's cottage cooking pasta."

"Nick walked out on Spielberg for me."

"Gabe was going to quit the race for DA."

"Jace took me to Fright Fest," Noelle muttered, staring at her lap.

"He what?" Devin scrunched up her nose.

"Smuggled me out of Spaulding and brought me to a horror film festival in Phoenix so I could meet John Carpenter."

"Ohmigod, Noe," Holly squealed. "How did he find out?"

"Find out what?" Devin asked.

"Noelle is a closet horror movie fanatic," Ivy answered. "She can't get enough of 'em."

"He dug up an interview I gave to some small weekly newspaper about a million years ago." Noelle rested her back against a potting bench and sighed. "I think that's when I started falling for him."

"So you have fallen for him." Holly tilted her head and squinted, the better to study her youngest sibling. "Is the feeling mutual?"

"I don't know." Noelle twisted the hem of her peasant blouse into a ball. "He said he wants to be more than friends. I'm just not sure how much more."

Ivy traced the outline of one of the paving stones with the toe of her electric purple Chuck Taylor. "As a wise French man once told me when I was in a similar situation with Cade, there's only one way to find out."

"What's that?"

"Ask him, *ma chére*," Ivy said in her best cheesy French accent.

"Easier said than done when he's on the other side of the country." Noelle fingered the velvety, fragrant bloom of a crimson-tipped, pale peach rose on the bottom shelf of the potting bench. No doubt another one of her father's hybrids. "It's not exactly the kind of thing I can ask in a phone call or on Skype."

"When will you see him next?" Devin asked.

"Another thing I don't know." There seemed to be a lot of that going around. "He's dealing with some family stuff right now. That's why he went home."

Noelle left it at that, not wanting to betray Jace's confidence. She'd been scouring the internet, but somehow he'd managed to keep his dad's arrest quiet. And she wasn't going to be the one to change that by shooting her mouth off. Not even to the people closest to her.

"Okay." Holly rubbed her hands together. "Time for plan B."

"Do I want to know what that is?" Noelle asked.

"You may have to wait to find out Mr. MVP's intentions, but that doesn't mean you can't use your absence to make his heart grow a little fonder." Holly turned to Ivy, the expression on her face somewhere between gleeful and gloating. "You said something about boudoir photos?"

Ivy high-fived her older sister. "Hell, yeah."

"Hell, no." Noelle crossed her arms in front of her chest. "I'm not an exhibitionist."

"I promise they'll be tasteful," Ivy assured her. "High-end lingerie. No nudity. For Jace's eyes only."

Okay, Noelle was tempted. Racy pictures would be a big hit with Jace. And she owed him for the care package he'd sent her, which had arrived just before she left Arizona—the entire *Evil Dead* series on DVD, the soundtrack from *A Nightmare on Elm Street*, a collection of Stephen King short stories and a pair of plastic vampire teeth. But the risk of photos accidentally falling into the wrong hands was too great. Unless...

"No lingerie," she said after a long moment's consideration. "But I saw a website once of this photographer who specialized in recreating old pinup shots. You know, vintage clothing. Period hair and makeup. Think you can do something like that?"

Ivy's eyes sparked at the challenge. "We'd have to put together a wardrobe for you. But I don't see why not. Sounds like fun."

"Great." Noelle clapped her hands and eyed the door. "When can we get started?"

16

JACE TURNED THE key in his lock for the first time in over a month and pushed the door open, relieved to be greeted by the smell of lemon Pledge and not musty gym socks, courtesy of his cleaning service. He tossed his keys on the kitchen counter, noting the neat piles of mail stacked according to type—bills, catalogs, letters, junk mail. Why didn't he have his agent handle this crap?

Oh, well. He'd have to deal with it sooner or later, and he had an hour or so to kill while his dad was at Gamblers Anonymous. More than enough time to at least weed through and grab the important stuff to read later.

He opened the fridge, hoping to find some decent beer to make the drudgery of going through mail slightly more bearable. He'd left town so fast he couldn't remember what state his refrigerator was in. Who was he kidding? He was a single guy. His fridge only had two states: empty and nothing but beer. He had a fifty-fifty shot of getting lucky.

Jackpot.

He snagged an IPA from the top shelf, opened it and took a deep chug before pulling up a stool and confronting the mail. Most of it he was able to chuck in the circu-

lar file. The rest he stuffed in a grocery bag to go through later with the exception of two things that caught his eye, one that looked to be a card and the other a thick overnight envelope, both with unfamiliar return addresses.

He tore the card open first. The front had a picture of a stick figure in a backward ball cap and the words "You rock, bro." Jace flipped it open, his eyes immediately going to the signature at the bottom. Dylan Young. It took a second for the name to register, and when it did he felt as worthless as dog shit on the bottom of a shoe.

Dylan. The kid at rehab. Jace had left so fast he hadn't even had a chance to stay goodbye. Something that hadn't even occurred to him until now. Making him a selfish bastard six times over, no matter how bad the situation with his dad had been.

He suppressed the desire to slam his good hand on the counter and instead read the note Dylan had written inside the card.

Dear Mr. Morgan,

  I mean Jace LOL. Noelle told me you had to check out of Spaulding early because of a family emergency. I hope everything is okay. And I hope it's okay that she gave me your address. I just wanted to say thanks for giving me all that stuff about Jim Abbott and Pete Gray. I don't know if I'll ever be as good as them, but at least now I know I can try. I'm going home tomorrow, but my email and phone number are at the bottom of this card. My mom says if you're ever in Flagstaff she'll cook you the best meal of your life.

  Peace out,
  Dylan Young

P.S. Thank Reid and Cooper for all the great Storm gear, especially the signed jersey.

P.P.S. She means it about the meal. My mom is mad awesome in the kitchen.

Jace chuckled as he folded the card and put it in his back pocket. The kid might be minus an arm, but with that attitude he was going to go places. Jace made a mental note to call him as soon as he got his dad back home.

Next up: the overnight envelope. He pulled the tab across the top, opening the seal, and reached in to slide out...

Hell fucking yeah. Photo after photo of Noelle in an array of outfits that didn't reveal much in the way of skin but were still sexy as all get-out. Form-fitting, cropped jeans with a Daisy Duke style halter top and cherry red do-me heels. A 1950s inspired dress with some sort of Hawaiian flower tucked behind one ear. What looked like mechanic's coveralls, unzipped enough to show a yellow-and-white checked bikini top.

And that wasn't even the half of it. Each photo seemed to get hotter than the last. She was the perfect pinup girl, with her ruby lips and her hair in loose, full curls that fell to her shoulders. He stared at the pictures for a good five minutes with his mouth open and his dick straining against his fly before coherent thought returned.

He fished his cell phone out of his pocket with the other and headed for his bedroom, dialing Noelle's number as he went.

"Hey," a tired voice greeted him. "I just got home. I was going to call you after I had some dinner."

He sat on the bed and glanced at the clock on his nightstand. Four-thirty in the afternoon, which meant seven-

thirty at night in New York. "Right, the time difference. Want to call me back when you're done?"

"No." She sighed, long and deep, vibrating across the airwaves and ending in a sexy moan that had his dick practically popping out of his pants. "I'm glad you called. I needed to hear your voice right about now."

He adjusted his zipper and tried to focus on what she was saying and not his raging hard-on. "Bad day?"

"That's an understatement."

"Want to talk about it?"

"Later." She sighed again and he could see her, head back, eyes closed, phone in one hand and the other rubbing her feet, stiff and sore from hours of dancing. In his mind's eye, his hands replaced hers, soothing away all her aches and pains. When she was totally relaxed, they'd order in some Thai food, maybe binge-watch *Arrow* on Netflix and eventually make their way to the bedroom where they'd…

"First I want to hear about your day." Her voice snapped him out of his fantasy. Just when it was getting good. Damn shame.

He shook his head to bring him fully back to the present and stretched out on the bed. "Nothing special until I opened my mail a few minutes ago."

"Oh?" The single word was loaded with uncertainty, which only made him want her more.

"I got some…interesting photos." He fanned them out on the bed next to him, his fingers itching with the need to touch the real her, not an ink-and-paper facsimile. "You wouldn't know anything about that, would you?"

"Interesting, huh?" He could almost hear her biting her lip like she did when she was nervous. "Good interesting or bad interesting?"

"Definitely good. Very, very good."

"I wasn't sure you'd like them. Ivy said guys are into that kind of stuff but…"

"If I liked them any more I'd have shot my load in my tighty whities." He massaged his aching dick through his jeans, an idea forming in his one-track mind. "What are you wearing now?"

"Nothing like in the pictures. Baggy shorts. Tank top. A Band-Aid on every toe."

He smiled. "I can work with that."

"Did I mention that the shorts have a rip on the butt? And the top's soaked through with sweat."

"Even better."

"Very funny."

"I'm totally serious. You could be in a burlap sack and I'd be turned on."

"Maybe I should have worn that for the photo shoot. It would have been cheaper. And more comfortable."

"Next time." He unzipped his jeans and lifted his hips to shove them—and his underwear—down far enough to free his throbbing cock. He wrapped his hand around the base and gave it a slow, measured stroke, needing to pace himself. They might be miles apart, but he'd make damned sure they came together. "Right now I want you to do something for me."

"What?" She sounded breathless, like she knew what he was about to ask.

"Touch yourself."

"Where?"

"Wherever it feels good." He stroked himself again, faster this time. "Are you doing it?"

"Yes."

He could hear rustling and pictured her opening her legs and slipping her free hand under the waistband of